A SHOT AT THE GUNSMITH

Kennedy looked at Rigg with distaste. "I didn't hire you to go up against the Gunsmith. I need somebody who won't start sweating at the sound of his name."

Self-consciously, Rigg wiped his sleeve across his forehead. "Who you got in mind?"

"You ever hear of Trey Hatcher?"

"Hatcher!" Rigg said. "Sure, he's got a big rep—do you think you can get him?"

"Hell yes, I can get him," Kennedy said. "He's old enough to be smart, but young enough to want a shot at the Gunsmith."

"Will he be good enough?" Rigg asked.

Kennedy rubbed his chin. "Well, that's something we'll all have to find out, isn't it?"

The Gunsmith by J.R. Roberts

THE GUNSMITH

#110

WYOMING RANGE WAR

SPEAKING VOLUMES, LLC
NAPLES, FLORIDA
2015

THE GUNSMITH
#110 WYOMING RANGE WAR

ISBN 978-1-61232-713-6

THE GUNSMITH

#110

WYOMING RANGE WAR

J.R. ROBERTS

Chapter One

Beverly Press held a very special place in the heart of Clint Adams.

When Clint had needed help, she came through for him, and at *that* time she didn't even know him very well.* It was the time that Duke was missing and Clint needed a decent horse to ride while he searched for him. Clint valued nothing higher than the big black gelding, and Beverly Press put a high price on her white stallion, Lancelot. Still, she loaned Clint big Lance, not once, but twice, the second time when Clint had to search for the man who had shot Duke, almost killing him. Lancelot—or Lance, as Clint called him—was the only horse Clint had ever found who was even *close* to Duke.

And he had found very few women who came close to Beverly Press, as a woman and as a friend.

Since he thought so much of her, whenever he

_____
*THE GUNSMITH #28

was within hailing distance of her Wyoming ranch, he stopped by.

He had stopped in three days before, and ten minutes after his arrival, they were in her bed.

They were in her bed now, on the third morning, and she was down between his legs, waking him up in the nicest way possible.

"Hey," he said.

She looked up at him and allowed his erect penis to slide free of her mouth. It throbbed, glistening with her saliva.

"Good morning," she said, smiling widely.

"That's all I've had the past three days."

"Days?"

"And nights."

"They can get better."

"I thought you had to go out of town."

"I do," she said, wrapping her thumb and forefinger around the base of his cock, "but you *could* be here when I get back."

"Beverly . . ."

"I know," she said. "Relax . . . I know."

She moved up onto him, and he cupped her broad butt as she lowered herself onto him, taking him inside of her. He reached up and cupped her firm breasts, tweaking the nipples with his thumbs. For a woman in her early forties, she had an incredible body, smooth and firm, showing only a hint of wear in a slight thickening of her waist and hips.

"Mmm," she moaned, reaching down and placing the flat of her palms against his chest. As she continued to ride him up and down, she scraped his chest with her nails.

He ran his hands around her side and up her back, pulling her down so that she was lying over him, her breasts flattened against his chest. She covered his mouth with hers, sliding her tongue between his lips. He ran his hands down her back, cupping her buttocks again, and they moved together until she moaned into his mouth, just seconds before he exploded inside of her. . . .

"I meant what I said, you know."

"Which time?" he asked, smiling at her.

They were at the dining-room table, having breakfast.

"About you staying here."

"I've told you, Beverly—"

"I'm not asking you to marry me, you dope," she said. "You said yourself you were worn out. Just because I have to go on a business trip doesn't mean you have to move on."

She did have a point. He wanted to rest, and this was a better place than most to do so.

"In fact," she said, "I have some neighbors who'd like to meet you."

"Oh?"

"Yes," she said, "new neighbors. They bought the ranch adjacent to mine to the east of here."

"*They?* More than one owner? That's always asking for trouble."

"You'll find this situation even more unusual than most."

Clint frowned at her.

"What have you got up your sleeve, Beverly?"

"Nothing," she said, her face glowing with innocence. "I just want you to meet some friends, that's all."

"Sure," Clint said, "that's all."

After breakfast, Clint and Beverly went to the stable to saddle their horses.

"Look at those two," he said as they entered.

Duke and Lance were stabled across from each other, and both were holding their heads high, staring at each other.

"What would have happened if we had put them side by side?" she asked.

"I don't even want to think about it," Clint said.

He took Duke out and saddled him, while Beverly saddled her mare.

"You still don't ride him?" Clint asked, pointing to Lancelot.

She shook her head. "You and my late husband are still the only two who ever have."

Clint shook his head, and they walked their mounts outside.

"These friends of yours," Clint asked after they had mounted up, "are they in trouble?"

She hesitated before answering. "They're having some . . . difficulties."

"Are you sure you didn't set this up?"

"How could I have?" she asked. "I didn't know you were coming, did I?"

"No," he admitted, "but I have the uncomfortable feeling that I'm being suckered into something. Remember, I came here to rest."

"Oh, you'll rest," she assured him. "In fact, you'll probably get more rest with me gone than you would if I was still here."

Remembering their last three nights together, he said, "That's for sure."

During the ride to her "friends'" ranch, Clint couldn't pry loose any information *about* the friends in question. That made him all the more curious about them.

"There's the house," Beverly finally said.

Most of the distance they had covered from house to house had been land owned by Beverly. Clint wasn't sure when they had crossed the border between the two ranches, but he was sure it couldn't have been very far back.

"Not much of a ranch," he observed.

"Maybe not compared to mine," she said, "but with a little work . . ."

To Clint the place looked like it needed more than "just a little work." The corral was in pieces, while the house needed a coat of paint and some serious carpentry repairs.

"When did these friends of yours take this place over?" he asked.

"About three months ago."

"And this is all they've done?"

She smiled. "You should have seen the place three months ago."

"I think I'm glad I never did," he said.

They rode up to the front of the house and dismounted. As they did so, the front door opened. A woman carrying a rifle stepped out. She was tall, rangy, and red-haired, apparently in her thirties. She wore no make-up, but Clint could see she was a handsome woman. She strongly resembled a Beverly Press of ten years before.

"Your friend?" Clint asked her.

"Wait," Beverly said.

Another woman stepped out of the doorway and stood next to the first one. She held a handgun in her right hand, though she was obviously uncomfortable with it. She had very black hair and very large brown eyes. She was not as tall as the first woman but as slender. She appeared to be in her late twenties.

"Your friends, I presume," Clint said.

Beverly smiled and said, "Wait."

He frowned, turning back to look at the house.

They came out of the house in quick succession then: another woman, younger than the other two, so young that she could have been the first woman's daughter—and probably was; a fourth woman, blond and full-bodied, probably in her mid to late thirties; a woman who was more girl than woman, no more than seventeen or eighteen, brown-haired and wide-eyed; and finally a woman who was at least fifty, perhaps more. Her dark hair was streaked with gray, but she carried herself stiffly and proudly erect, and she was still a good-looking woman.

"Is that all?" Clint asked, looking at Beverly.

"Clint," she said, smiling broadly, "meet my friends."

Chapter Two

Six women, all from the east, had come west to leave their lives behind them and start new ones. They had pooled their money and bought this ranch. Beverly had met two of them in town, then met the other four, and she had become friendly enough with them that she was trying to help them.

To that end, she had now introduced them to Clint Adams.

"Clint is going to be staying at my place for a while," Beverly said, "while I'm away on business."

"Is that so?" asked the first woman, who had stepped out of the house carrying the rifle. Her name was Angela Dennison. Clint had correctly identified one of the younger women as Angela's daughter, Irene. There seemed to be less than twenty years between them.

The women had invited Beverly and Clint in for coffee, and they were all crowded into the small kitchen area.

"I've been helping Angela and the girls as much as I can," Beverly explained to Clint. "They don't know much about ranching."

"Beverly's been a life-saver," Irene Dennison said. She had been staring at Clint since he entered the house with Beverly.

"She's been a big help, all right," Angela added.

The other women nodded their agreement.

The black-haired woman was named Sandra Ward. The oldest of the six women was Alice Williams. The blonde was Katy Brennan, and the youngest of the women was seventeen-year-old Bonnie Franks. Rather than boldly stare at him the way Irene Dennison did, Bonnie was sneaking glances at him from time to time. In one form or another, he was getting the once-over from each of the women. Some of it was interest, some curiosity. Clint was struck by the fact that all of the women were extremely attractive.

The women seemed to leave the talking to Angela Dennison, so until he was proved wrong, Clint decided that she was their leader.

"This is good coffee," he said, for want of something else to say, even though it was a lie.

"All right," said Beverly, "I guess I should tell you all why I brought Clint here."

"It would be nice," Angela said.

"I just wanted you all to meet," she said, "since he'll be staying at my place for a while."

"To rest," Clint added.

"Yes, of course," Beverly said. "To rest."

"From what?" Angela asked. "I mean, what is your business, Mr. Adams?"

"I'm a gunsmith."

"I see," said Angela. "Well, we really don't need the services of a gunsmith right now."

"And I don't know all that much about ranching."

Angela stared at Clint. "I don't see that we have much in common, then."

"I guess not," Clint agreed.

"Clint," Beverly said, "could you step outside for a minute?"

"Sure." Truth be told, he was glad to get away from the six pairs of eyes that were boring into him. "I'll wait right outside."

He left the house. He still didn't know why Beverly had brought him over here, and he wondered if she knew herself.

"What's wrong with you, Angela?" Beverly asked.

"What do you mean?"

"You know what I mean!" said Beverly. "That man is a good friend of mine, and you treated him shabbily."

"Did I?"

"You know you did."

"Well," Angela said, "he is *your* friend, not mine."

"What's that got to do with it?" demanded Beverly. "He was a guest here. Do you treat all your guests like that?"

"No," Irene Dennison said, "only the men."

"Irene!" said Angela sharply.

"Is that it?" Beverly asked. "You treated him badly because he's a man?"

"It's as good a reason as any," Angela replied.

Beverly looked at the other women, who all found something else to look at.

"Well," she said helplessly, "I don't know what you're all running from, and I guess I don't have any right to ask."

"That's right," Angela said, "you don't. We appreciate the help you've given us, Beverly, but that doesn't mean we have to accept anything you want to cram down our throats."

"She can cram *him* down *my* throat any time," Katy Brennan said. Nobody laughed, and Angela gave her a dirty look.

Beverly stood up. "I guess I'd better go."

She turned and was out the door when Irene Dennison stood up. "Oh, Mother!" she said, and she went after Beverly.

"Beverly?"

Clint was standing with the horses, and Beverly had been walking toward him when she heard Irene calling to her.

Beverly stopped and waited for Irene to catch up to her.

"Please," Irene said, taking hold of Beverly's arm, "don't hold my mother's hatred of men against her."

"I couldn't do that if I wanted to, Irene," Beverly said. "Not unless I knew what was behind it."

Irene looked at the ground. "I can't tell you that."

"I'm not asking you to, Irene." Beverly gave the young girl a hug. "I'm leaving tomorrow, but I'll be back next month."

"Thanks for all your help," Irene said. "And tell your friend it was a pleasure to meet him."

"I'll tell him," Beverly promised.

•   •   •

"I'm sorry for the way they treated you," Beverly said in bed that night.

"They were all right," Clint said.

"Except Angela."

Clint shrugged. "Maybe she just doesn't like men."

"What makes you say that?"

He shrugged again. "I don't know. It was just the impression I got."

"Well, I'm afraid you're right," Beverly said. "I wish I knew why."

"Who knows?" Clint said. "It might have something to do with her husband, Irene's father."

"I suppose," Beverly said. "The others liked you, though."

"Did they?"

"Oh, come on," she said. "Don't tell me you didn't feel them devouring you with their eyes."

"Mmmm . . . no, I didn't feel it."

"Liar," she said, slapping his shoulder.

"Besides," he said, "if I'm going to be devoured, I'd rather it be by something other than a woman's eyes."

"Is that a hint, sir?"

"If you take it as one."

She thought it over for a few moments, then slipped beneath the sheets, which muffled her voice as she said, "I think I will."

He felt her tongue moving over him, her hands cupping him, and then her mouth coming down over him, literally devouring him. He was sorry she was leaving the next day, as he had not yet decided if he was going to stay on or not after she was gone.

However, that was a decision he could not concentrate on making. Not at that exact moment, that is.

Chapter Three

Little Creek, Wyoming, had grown since Clint had last seen it. It looked as if it was a town definitely on the rise. All it lacked to really make it grow was a railroad station.

Clint rode into town with Beverly to see her off on the stagecoach. Rather than have lunch at the house, Clint told her he'd buy her a big breakfast at the hotel to send her off.

"Have you decided what you want to do?" she asked.

"About what?"

"About staying at my place for a while."

"Oh, that," he said. "I meant to think about it overnight, but, if you recall, you didn't give me much time to think."

"Why is this such a major decision for you?" she asked.

"I came here to see you, Beverly," Clint said. "We didn't spend as much time together as I would have liked. You're leaving now, and there's really no reason for me to stay."

"You'll have the whole place to yourself," she said, "and you can rest. I've already told Pevy that you might be staying." Pevy was her foreman.

"Pevy doesn't like me."

"You seem to have trouble with my foremen, don't you?"

Years before, when they had first met, her foreman's name was Meade, and he and Clint had gotten off on the wrong foot immediately.

"As long as I don't have trouble with you," Clint said.

"That won't ever happen," she said. "Not if you keep feeding me like this, that is."

"I'd go broke if I had to feed you every day."

She kicked him under the table.

Later, they embraced for the last time before she boarded the stage.

"Look," she said, before getting into the coach, "stay at my place or don't, but the way some of those friends of mine were looking you over, I doubt that you'll be alone for very long."

"Is that a fact?"

She kissed his cheek and boarded the stage. She waved once from the window, and then the coach was gone and he was alone.

He thought for a moment about going back to the ranch, but all he had waiting for him there was Pevy. He decided to go and have a beer and finally make up his mind about whether he was coming or going.

Chapter Four

Katy Brennan and Bonnie Frank rode into town on their battered buckboard later that afternoon.

As they got down, Katy said to Bonnie, "Now stay away from the men in town while I'm in the general store."

"That's not funny, Katy."

"Take it easy, Bonnie," Katy said. "Don't be so thin-skinned all the time."

"I'll come with you."

"Fine," Katy said, "come on. I want to get back before dinner."

"We should have come in this morning," Bonnie said. "Then we could have been home by lunch."

"You know my hair was wet this morning, Bonnie," Katy said. "Let's go."

It took Clint two beers to decide that he was going to leave Little Creek, and Beverly's ranch, and move on. He just didn't feel like staying in Beverly's big house without her. Also, he didn't relish having to constantly deal with Pevy's dirty looks. It would be better for him to move on and find someplace else to light for a while.

He contemplated a third beer, then decided he'd be better off riding back to the ranch to pack his things and get his rig. He'd take a room at the hotel for the night, and in the morning he'd be on his way.

Teddy Rigg and Frank Lobo were sitting in chairs across the street from the general store when Katy Brennan and Bonnie Franks rode in.

"Lookee here!" Rigg said.

"Cute," Lobo said.

"I'm talking about the big blonde," Rigg said, licking his lips.

"I'm talking about the young one," Lobo said. "I like little young ones."

"All right," Rigg said, "I'll take the blonde and you take the young one."

"Let's go." Lobo began getting out of his seat.

"Not yet," Rigg said, putting his hand on his partner's arm. "Let's wait until they come out. They'll need help carrying their packages."

"We gotta carry their packages?" Lobo asked.

"Just do what I tell you," Rigg said, "and you'll have your little one right where you want her."

When Katy and Bonnie came out of the store, each was carrying a box of supplies. Before they could lay them on the flat of the buckboard, two men were at their sides.

"Need some help, ladies?" one of them asked. He was tall, with a sallow complexion and long, stringy hair.

"Not really," Katy said.

"Aw, come on," the other man said. He was shorter and stockier than the other, but they both had something in common: They smelled bad.

"Please," Bonnie said as the stocky man grabbed her box.

"I'm just trying to help, little lady," the man said, leaning close. His breath was so bad that she recoiled from it.

He put the box on the buckboard while the other man took Katy's box and did the same.

"Thanks a lot," Katy said. "Come on, Bonnie."

Katy took Bonnie's arm, but the stocky man grabbed her other arm.

"Hey, what's the hurry?" he said.

"Please let go of her," Katy said.

"Relax, sweetheart," the other man said. "We just want a little thank-you for our help."

"I thanked you."

The man with the stringy hair moved closer to Katy and roughly took hold of one of her breasts. "Not the way I like to be thanked."

"Hey!" She began squirming, but he was holding her tight.

"Oh, Frank, you gotta feel this!" he said, squeezing her harder.

"I got my own," Lobo said, sliding his arm around Bonnie's small waist.

"Let go!" Bonnie shouted, but the more she struggled, the tighter Frank Lobo held her.

"Does the other one feel as good?" Teddy Rigg asked Katy.

"Forget it, mister," Katy said, and she stomped on the man's instep.

Rigg howled in pain, releasing Katy's breast and reaching for his foot. As she tried to move away from him, however, he reached out with his other hand and backhanded her. She staggered backward, and her heels struck the boardwalk behind her, tumbling her onto her back.

"Katy!" Bonnie shouted.

"Don't worry, honey," Lobo said. "I'm gonna take better care of you."

Chapter Five

Clint stepped out of the saloon in time to see Katy Brennan go tumbling backward. As he watched, he saw another man lift Bonnie Franks completely off her feet, laughing while he was doing it. The man who had knocked Katy Brennan down was bent over, rubbing his foot.

Clint started across the street, and as he did so the man with the stringy hair reached down, took hold of the front of Katy's shirt, and hauled her to her feet.

"Let them go!" Clint said as he reached the buckboard.

Both men stopped to look at him.

"Get lost, cowboy," the man with the stringy hair said. He still had a handful of Katy's shirt.

"Not until you let her go," Clint said. He looked at the other man and added, "You too, friend. Let her go . . . now!"

Lobo frowned, but he lowered Bonnie to her feet

and loosened his hold on her enough so that she was able to pull away.

"Teddy . . ." Lobo said.

"Don't worry, Frank," Rigg said. "This feller's not here to ruin our fun. . . .Are you, friend? You wanna turn right around and go back to the saloon, don't you?"

"No."

"If I was you," Rigg said, "that's what I'd do."

"If I were you," Clint said, "I'd get my hands off the lady."

Frowning now, Rigg released Katy so abruptly that she staggered back a step and almost went down again. She regained her balance and hurried over to where Bonnie was standing. Clint saw the older woman push the younger one into a new position, where they wouldn't be in the way.

"Now, friend—" Rigg started, but Clint interrupted him.

"I'm not your friend," he said, "and I don't think that there's any danger of me ever becoming your friend. Now that you've let the ladies go, I'd advise you to move on."

"You'd 'advise' us . . ." Rigg looked at his partner and said, "Frank, this feller needs to be taught some manners. You up to it?"

Lobo grinned. "I sure am."

Rigg looked at Clint and asked, "You want gunplay, or will you take it this way?"

"Gunplay would only leave the two of you dead," Clint said confidently. He turned to Frank Lobo. "Come ahead, then."

"This won't take long, Teddy," Lobo said. "Don't let the women leave."

"They won't go far," Rigg promised. "Get 'im, Frank!"

Frank Lobo was so confident that he just walked up to Clint and threw one punch, as if Clint would just stand there and let it land. Clint sidestepped the blow and drove his left fist into the man's midsection. Lobo stopped, stunned by the blow, and Clint hit him on the side of his face with a right that drove the man to his knees. Clint stepped past the man then, measured him, and kicked him in the back of the head. Lobo fell over and hit the ground face-first.

Clint turned just as Teddy Rigg was moving for his gun.

"You touch that gun and you're a dead man," he said loudly.

By now a small crowd had gathered around, and they were watching intently, waiting to see if blood were going to be spilled.

The force of Clint Adams's voice caused Teddy Rigg to reconsider drawing his gun.

"This ain't over, feller," Rigg said.

"It is for now," Clint said. "Pick up your friend and move on."

Teddy Rigg circled the buckboard and hauled Frank Lobo to his feet. Lobo's legs were rubbery, and Rigg had to half-walk, half-drag him away.

Clint stepped over to the two women and asked, "Are you all right?"

"Jesus!" Bonnie said.

"We are now!" Katy said. "Thanks to you."

"I don't think they'll bother you any more," Clint said.

"Not today, anyway," Katy said.

"Do you know who they are?"

She shook her head. "Never saw them before. We owe you a lot."

"Don't worry about it."

"I mean for yesterday as well as today," Katy said. "We didn't treat you very well."

"I figured you had your reasons."

"Some of us did," she said.

"Kate . . ." Bonnie began.

"Bonnie, don't you have to pick up some cloth from the dress shop?"

"Cloth?" Bonnie repeated, obviously confused.

"Mr. Adams, I'd appreciate it if you'd keep me company over a cup of coffee while Bonnie runs her errand."

"Errand?" Bonnie was still confused, since she had no further errands to run that she knew of.

"Well . . ." Clint said.

"You weren't in a hurry to go anywhere, were you?" Katy asked.

"Well, no, ma'am."

"Oh, please," she said, "call me Katy, and I'll pay for the coffee."

"There's no need for that."

"It's the least I can do," she said, "after what you just did for us."

"All right," Clint said with a shrug. "I can use a cup of coffee."

"Bonnie," Katy said to her confused friend, "I'll meet you right back here, okay?"

"Okay," Bonnie said, "but Katy, I don't have to go to the dress shop."

"You don't?"

"No."

"Well," Katy said, tossing Clint a sideways glance, "I could have sworn you *said* you had to."

"No," Bonnie said, shaking her head emphatically, "I never said—"

"Well then, why don't you just go over to Mrs. Livingston's house and have a cup of tea with her?" Katy suggested.

"Well," Bonnie said, "okay, I guess . . ."

"Mrs. Livingston's this nice old lady we know in town," Katy explained to Clint. "She likes one of us to look in on her whenever we're in town."

"I see," Clint said.

"Shall we go and have that cup of coffee?" Katy asked. "There's a small cafe just down the block."

Clint, a bit confused himself by the exchange between the two women, said, "Lead the way."

Chapter Six

They found a table in the Golden Nugget Cafe and ordered coffee and peach pie. The pie was ordered on Katy's recommendation, and she looked like a woman who knew good pie when she tasted it. In a few years Katy Brennan would find herself faced with a decision: stop eating or be fat. Right now she was well-fed, with full breasts and hips that caused men's heads to turn.

"I feel I should explain," Katy said.

"About what?"

"About the way Angela treated you yesterday."

"If she doesn't feel the need to explain, then you shouldn't."

She smiled.

"That's nice of you, but the fact remains she was horrible to you, and you didn't deserve it."

She had an accent that Clint couldn't quite identify. It was obvious that she and Angela Dennison—and probably the others—were not western women.

"New York?" he asked.

"What?"

"Are you all from New York?"

"Close," she said. "New Jersey, right across the East River."

"Ah."

"Have you been there?"

"To New Jersey? No, but I have been to New York," Clint said.

"What did you think of it?"

"I liked it, but after a while the city—any city—closes in on me."

"Where do you go when you feel like being in the city?" she asked.

"Usually to San Francisco. I have friends there."

"I'll bet you have friends in a lot of places."

"What makes you say that?"

"Well, if you're as helpful everywhere as you were with us . . . I mean, you didn't *have* to step in when you did. That's sort of buying into someone else's trouble, isn't it?" she asked.

"It is," he said, "and you're right, I do that a lot. I suppose I have a lot of friends as a result of it—or acquaintances—but it also works the other way."

"What way?"

"I end up with a lot of enemies, as well."

They finished their coffee and pie, and then Clint took out some money.

"Oh, no," she protested, "I'm paying, remember?"

"That's all right," he said, putting the money on the table. "You can pay next time."

"Sure," she said, smiling at him. "I'll bet you never let a woman pay for anything."

He just smiled as they stood up.

They left the cafe and started walking back to the buckboard, where Bonnie would be waiting for Katy, but as they came to the mouth of an alley Katy suddenly shifted her weight into Clint, pushing him into the alley itself.

Before he realized what was happening, she had him pinned to the wall with her body. She slid her hands behind his neck, pulled his face down to hers, and kissed him, open-mouthed. She pushed her tongue into his mouth and moaned, pressing her firm body against him. The pressure of her hips and abdomen was insistent, and he slid his hands down her back to cup her generous backside, pulling her even more tightly to him.

When she pulled her mouth from his, she was gasping and breathing heavily.

"What was that for?" he asked.

"Well, you wouldn't let me pay for the coffee," she said, "so I had to think of *some* way to thank you for what you did."

He was about to speak when she kissed him again, this time longer, rubbing herself against him the whole time. He found no reason to protest, so he threw himself into the spirit of the kiss. He slid one hand between them and cupped one of her breasts, his other hand massaging her ass. He could feel the hard nipple right through her clothes, and this time when she moaned it was more like a groan.

"Jesus!" she said, breaking the kiss. "I wish we had time to go to the hotel so I could thank you properly."

She kissed him again, and Clint found himself wishing the same thing.

"Wouldn't Bonnie wonder what happened to you?" he asked, between kisses.

At the mention of Bonnie, Katy backed up and stared at him. She was breathing hard, and her eyes seemed to be a little out of focus.

"Yes," she said, "she would, damn it." As he watched, she regained her composure, her eyes coming into focus, her breathing slowing down.

"Are you staying at Beverly's ranch?" she asked him.

"Well . . ."

"I'll come to you there," she said, moving away from him. "I have to get back now, but I'll come to the ranch tonight."

"Katy—"

"I'll see you then, Clint." She kissed him again. It was meant to be a short kiss, but once her lips touched his it was as if they had become fused together. Finally, reluctantly, she pulled her mouth free and hurried away.

Clint stepped out of the alley and watched her as she ran toward the buckboard. Bonnie was waiting. It looked as if she started to ask Katy some questions, but Katy brushed them off. They both climbed aboard the buckboard and rode out of town.

Clint himself was a little out of breath after the encounter with Katy Brennan, but he found himself thinking that maybe it *would* be a good idea to stay at Beverly's, if just for a few days.

Rigg and Lobo watched as the two women rode out of town. Lobo was still rubbing the back of his head, where Clint had kicked him.

"Those women are from the old Beckett place, aren't they?" Rigg asked.

"I guess."

"There's a bunch of them out there," Rigg said. "That's what Mr. Kennedy said."

"Uh huh."

"You suppose he's gonna turn us loose on them women?" Rigg asked.

"He wants that ranch," Lobo said.

"Well then, maybe we ought to go and tell him that we made contact, huh?"

"What about that feller?" Lobo asked.

"The one who knocked you out with no trouble?" Rigg sneered.

"I can take him," Lobo insisted. "All I need's another chance."

"Well, maybe when we tell Mr. Kennedy that those women have hired themselves a gun, you'll get that chance."

"We don't know that they hired him," Lobo said, looking confused.

"No," Rigg said, "and we don't know that he's even a hired gun, but what does that matter? Come on, we got to get back to Mr. Kennedy's place. He's gonna want to make some plans."

Chapter Seven

When Clint got back to the ranch, Pevy was standing on the porch. Clint ignored the foreman and took Duke to the barn, taking his time unsaddling and settling him. When he returned to the house, Pevy was still on the porch.

Pevy was a big, competent-looking man with wide shoulders and large hands. He'd been working for Beverly Press for about twelve years, the last two as her foreman. He and Clint had never had that much contact, but it was plain in the way Pevy looked at him that the man didn't like him. Clint, on the other hand, had no real feelings about Pevy one way or the other.

"Pevy," he said in greeting, ascending the steps to the porch.

"You stayin'?" Pevy asked, getting right to the point.

Clint stopped to face the man. "For a while," he said finally. "Maybe."

31

"Don't get in my way."

"Why would I want to get in your way, Pevy?" Clint asked.

"You're Mrs. Press's guest, so I'll tolerate you," Pevy said, "but if you get in my way I'll put you off the property."

Clint bristled at the man's words. "Do you think you could, Pevy?" he asked. "Do you really think you could?"

Clint and Pevy glared at each other for a few moments, and it was the burly foreman who backed down.

"Just don't get in my way," he said, before walking down the steps.

Clint stared after the man until he had disappeared behind the barn. Then he used the key Beverly had left him to open the front door.

Once inside, he moved his gear out of Beverly's room and into one of the guest rooms. If Katy Brennan was really coming to see him that night, he certainly wasn't going to use Beverly's own room and bed.

When he came back downstairs the cook, Mrs. Marshall, asked him if he would like some dinner. She was a good-natured woman in her sixties who was one of the best cooks Clint had ever encountered.

"It's a little early, Mrs. Marshall, thank you," he said. "In fact, why don't you take the night off. If I get hungry I can fix myself something."

"Really, sir?"

"Sure," he said. "I'm sure you've got something else you'd rather do than cook me dinner."

"Well," the woman said, "I could spend some time with my mister."

"You do that, Mrs. Marshall," Clint said. "You go and spend the evening with your mister."

"Thank you, Mr. Adams," she said. "Thank you."

"You go ahead, Mrs. Marshall. Come back tomorrow afternoon."

"I can come and make you breakfast."

"You come back in the afternoon," Clint said. "Sleep late tomorrow."

"I haven't slept late in years!" Mrs. Marshall laughed, as if doing so were some forbidden vice.

Clint saw Mrs. Marshall off, assuring her that he could fix his own dinner when the time came.

When the time did come, he went to the kitchen and was about to make himself some eggs when there was a knock at the door. At that moment he felt a hint of guilt at the thought that it might be Katy Brennan, but then he remembered what Beverly had said before she left, about his not being alone while she was gone.

He left the kitchen and went to the front door. When he opened it, he found himself looking at a man, not at Katy Brennan.

"Can I help you?"

"Is Mrs. Press here?"

"No, she's not."

"Who are you?"

Clint stared at the man and asked, "Who are you?"

"My name is Tom Kennedy," the man said. "I'm a neighbor of Mrs. Press's."

"I see."

"Who are you?"

"My name is Clint Adams. I'm a friend of Beverly's."

"I see."

Tom Kennedy was a tall, well-dressed man in his early fifties, with dark hair gone silver at the temples. Clint wondered how well he and Beverly knew each other.

"Can I help you with something?"

"Are you . . . staying here?"

"For a while, perhaps," Clint said.

"I see."

"Well, I don't see," Clint said. "Why did you come here, Mr. Kennedy?"

"To see Mrs. Press, but, as she is not here, I suppose I'll be going."

"Don't let me stop you," Clint said. He didn't like the man at all. He had a feeling that he had come here for an entirely different reason.

"Good evening, Mr. Adams," Kennedy said. Clint watched as the man descended the steps, climbed into a buggy, and drove off.

Clint closed the door and turned to go back to the kitchen. He stopped short when he saw Katy Brennan standing by the stairs.

"What the—"

"Who was that?"

"A neighbor," he said.

"What did he want?"

"To see Beverly. How did you get in here?"

"I came in by the back. I didn't want anyone to see me."

"Why not?"

"I don't want the others to know I've been here."

"Why not?"

"I want it to be our secret."

It seemed to him that each answer led to another question, so he changed the subject.

"Are you hungry?" he asked. "I was about to fix something to eat."

"After," she said.

"After what?"

She turned, climbed three or four steps, looked at him over her shoulder, and said, "After."

Clint watched her until she had reached the top of the steps, out of sight. He started up then, saw her shirt come fluttering down the stairs, and quickened his pace.

When Tom Kennedy got back to his ranch, Rigg was waiting for him in the house. Kennedy walked past the man to his office, and Rigg followed.

"Shut the door," Kennedy said.

Rigg did so. "So?" he asked.

"You were right," Kennedy said. "He's staying at the Press ranch."

"Yeah, well, I knew I saw them together when she was gettin' on the stage. Who is he?"

"His name is Adams," Kennedy said, "Clint Adams. That ring a bell with you, Rigg?"

"Jesus!" Rigg said, stunned. "The Gunsmith!"

"You and Lobo are lucky to be alive."

"Jesus . . ." Rigg said again, wiping away the sweat that had suddenly come to his brow. "Is he working for them women?"

"I don't see how, if he's staying at the Press ranch," Kennedy said. "But I can't take any chances."

"What are you gonna do?"

"Send for help," Kennedy said.

"That's what you hired us for."

Kennedy looked at Rigg with distaste. "I didn't hire you to go up against the Gunsmith. That would be a waste of money. I need someone who won't start sweating at the sound of his name."

Self-consciously, Rigg wiped his sleeve across his forehead. "Who you got in mind?"

"I thought about it on the way back," Kennedy said. "You ever hear of Trey Hatcher?"

"Hatcher!" Rigg said. "Sure, he's got a big rep—"

"Not as big as the Gunsmith's," Kennedy admitted, "but Hatcher's only thirty."

"Do you think you can get him?"

"Hell yes, I can get him," Kennedy said. "He's old enough to be smart but young enough to want a shot at the Gunsmith. Yeah," Kennedy said again, sitting back in his chair, "I can get him."

"Will he be good enough?" Rigg asked.

Kennedy rubbed his chin. "Well, that's something we'll all have to find out, isn't it?"

Chapter Eight

She was waiting for him at the top of the stairs, naked to the waist. Her breasts were white, topped with dark brown nipples that were rigidly erect. He took her in his arms and kissed her. Her mouth was hungry—much hungrier than it had been in the alley earlier in the day. She kissed him, a long, deep, wet kiss that was almost desperate.

He broke the kiss so he could run his mouth over her breasts, and she let her head rock back on her neck. He held her by the small of the back, avidly kissing and sucking her nipples.

"Oh God!" she said. "Which room, quick!"

"Come on," he said.

He took her by the hand and led her to the guest room he was now using. Before they were inside she'd already begun to undress him. When she had his chest bare, she eagerly pressed herself to him, her nipples scraping his chest, her flesh burning his.

Clint got down on his knees, unbuttoned her pants,

and kissed her belly, licking her navel. He pulled her pants down to the floor, first removing her boots, and she stepped out of them. Next he relieved her of her underwear and then, still on his knees, he ran his tongue along her moist slit. Her taste was slightly bitter, her odor sharp, but he objected to neither.

"Oooh, my knees!" she moaned.

"What's wrong with your knees?"

"They're weak," she said. "It's been a long time between drinks, Clint."

"Well," he said, standing up, "let's move to the bed and you can drink your fill."

They walked to the bed, and while she reclined on it, he slipped off his boots and then his pants and joined her.

Her body was opulent, with big breasts and hips, a pillowy belly, full, almost chunky buttocks, and fleshy thighs—the kind of woman who was built for bed.

He straddled her quickly, and she reached between their bodies to grab his cock. She guided it to her wet slit, and he slid right in, swallowed whole by her.

If she had been eager and desperate before, she was pleading now.

"Oooh yes, please, hard, harder . . ." she gasped as he drove into her.

He strove to do her bidding, but as hard as he pounded into her, she wanted more. He slid his hands beneath her to grab her buttocks and pulled her to him with every thrust. Her powerful thighs were locked around him, and she was gasping into his ear, kissing his neck and shoulders, urging him on with her hands, running them over his back and ass, clutching him and then going crazy beneath him, bucking and yelling as she went over the edge, and he with her. . . .

"I guess I should have asked if there was anyone else in the house," she said later.

"Why?"

"Well," she said, "I know I'm kind of *loud*."

"Don't worry," he said. "I gave the cook the night off."

"Good."

"I was about to make some eggs before you got here," he said.

"Are you hungry?" she asked.

"More now than before," he said. "Exercise makes me hungry."

"I can make eggs," she said, bounding from the bed. Her breasts jiggled and slapped together for a moment.

"All right," he said, rising. He reached for his shirt, but she snatched it away from him.

"No clothes," she said.

"But—"

"What are you worried about, if the house is empty?" she asked, teasingly.

"I'm just not used to, uh, walking around naked."

"You have a good body," she said. "Slender but strong. Look at me: I'm about two or three meals away from chunky, and that's being kind."

"You have a fine body."

"If I can walk around naked, so can you," she said, ignoring his remark. She grabbed his hand. "Come on."

"All right," he said, "let's go and eat."

Chapter Nine

He sat in the kitchen and watched her prepare the eggs. Away from the bedroom, in the light of the kitchen, he could see that her thighs were too big, and her ass was getting there too, but in bed none of that mattered. So she'd never be skinny. Skinny women gave a man bone bruises in bed. Clint preferred women who were well padded and experienced, and Katy was both.

"Here we go," she said, setting a plate of eggs and potatoes in front of him. She'd had to search the kitchen for the utensils she needed, and when she found the potatoes she'd added them to the frying pan.

"Aren't you going to have any?" he asked.

"I'll pick at yours," she said, sitting across from him. "Go ahead. I want to watch you eat."

"Why?"

"You can learn a lot from watching the way a man eats," she said.

"Is that a fact?" he asked. "What did you learn this

afternoon, watching me eat the pie?"

"That you would be wonderful in bed."

"Is that right?"

"And I was right: You are," she said.

"So are you."

"I like it," she said. "That's why. I like sex more than anything."

"I could tell."

"I'm glad you could. You're an unusual man, Clint Adams."

"Why do you say that?"

"You made me happy—in bed, I mean. You were as concerned with my enjoyment as you were with your own. Believe me, that's rare."

"The more you enjoy it, the more I enjoy it," he said. "It's that simple."

"How are the eggs?" she asked.

"You were right," he said. "You *can* cook eggs."

"That's about all I can cook, so I'm glad you like it," she said.

He liked it fine. It was hard to ruin eggs anyway.

"Tell me something," he said.

"What?"

"Why did you all come here from New Jersey?"

"Well," she said, "first of all, we didn't leave New Jersey to come *here*. We just decided to come west and we ended up here."

"Why leave New Jersey?"

She made a face. "For a change."

The answer was evasive, but he decided not to press the issue.

"Do you know someone named Tom Kennedy?" he asked instead.

Suddenly, she didn't look so happy any more. "Why do you ask?"

"That's who was at the door when you got here."

"Do you know him?"

"Never met him before tonight," he said. "I can guess he's not one of your favorite people."

"Kennedy owns the ranch east of us."

"A big spread?"

"It wraps around ours and borders this one," she said. "It's big, all right. In fact, if he could swallow up our land, he'd have a bigger spread than Beverly."

Clint whistled. That would be a big spread.

"Are you having trouble with him?"

"Not yet," she said, "but we expect it. He wanted the Beckett place—that's what our place used to be called. We pooled our money and bought it. Later, he tried to buy it from us. We wouldn't sell, and he got real ugly."

"What did he offer you?"

"Double."

"And you didn't take it?"

"We didn't come here looking for money. We came looking for a place to live, and we found one."

"All of you together?"

"What's the matter?" she asked. "Don't you think six women can live together?"

"I guess."

"Sure, we have our problems," she said. "Angela's a little bossy—so's Alice, sometimes—Sandra's a little . . . But we get along . . . most of the time."

"So you turned down his offer?"

"Yes, and he said that wasn't the end of it. I'll bet those two men in town work for him."

"You think he's going to try and push you off?"

"That's what I think," she said. "What did he want here?"

"He said he was looking for Beverly," Clint said thoughtfully.

"You don't believe him?"

"I didn't feel he was being truthful at the time, and now I'm convinced."

"What do you think he wanted?"

"I think he wanted to find out who I was," Clint said. "If those men in town work for him and they told him what happened, he'd want to find out who I was."

"How'd he know you were here?"

"His men probably saw me put Beverly on the stage. He came over himself to see who I was."

"And?"

"And he found out."

"So?" she asked. "What does that mean?"

"It means I may end up causing you more trouble than I'm worth."

She frowned. "Why do you say that?"

"I have a certain . . . reputation, Katy."

"What kind?"

Briefly—as briefly as he could—he told her what his rep was.

"I see," she said. "So if he thinks that you're helping us or working for us . . . what?"

"He'll send for more help. Somebody better than those two in town today."

"A gunman?"

"Maybe."

"Maybe you should leave in the morning."

"I don't think so."

"Why not?"

"I want to find out first if I *have* caused you more trouble."

"Well," she said, "even if you have, it can't be more than you're worth."

"You don't think so?" he asked.

He had polished off the eggs and spuds by then, so she got up, came around to his side of the table, and slid onto his lap. His penis reacted immediately, swelling between them.

"I know so," she said.

He stood up, lifting her with him, and walked to the other end of the long wooden table, where it was empty, and set her down on it. She scooted forward a bit and spread her legs. He crouched between them and licked her.

"Oooh," she moaned.

"I can see," he said, "where it's an advantage to walk around naked."

Chapter Ten

"I have to go."

Katy got up from the bed and started getting dressed while Clint watched her.

"Why do you have to go?"

"I don't want the others to start wondering where I am."

"Why not?"

She finished dressing and looked down at Clint, a thoughtful expression on her face.

"We made certain agreements among ourselves when we left New Jersey."

"What kind of agreements?"

"No men."

"Are you the first to break that agreement?"

"I'm the only one to break it."

"Now I feel guilty."

She leaned over and kissed him. "Don't," she said. "It was a silly agreement, and I very much enjoyed breaking it with you."

"I enjoyed it, too."

"Now I really have to go," she said, moving toward the door.

"Where do they think you are?"

"Oh . . . out," she said. Then she left.

Clint placed his hands behind his head and looked up at the ceiling, wondering what he had gotten himself into.

When Katy Brennan got back to the house, she found Angela Dennison waiting for her on the front porch.

"You were with him, weren't you?"

"With who, dear?" Katy asked.

"You know who," Angela said. "Don't play games with me, Katy. Bonnie told me what happened in town."

"I had to thank him, Angela."

"We had an agreement."

"It was a silly agreement."

"You only think that because you can't be without a man for more than five minutes."

"I can be without a man, Angela," Katy said. "But I don't enjoy it, like you do, and I don't like being *forced* to be without a man."

Angela glared at her, silently fuming.

"We all have to live here together, Katy," Angela started to say, but Katy cut her off.

"We don't all have to live here together because *you* say we do, Angela," Katy said. "We all agreed to leave New Jersey and travel west, to get away from what we were and what we were doing."

"And now you're doing it again."

"I am not."

The two women faced each other for a few moments, and then Angela shook her head.

"We can't discuss this now," she said. "Let's get some sleep."

"I want to sit out here for a while."

"Suit yourself, Katy," Angela said. "You obviously intend to do the opposite of what I do."

"I intend to do what I want, Angela, not what you want. You want to live here and hide from men, that's your problem, not mine. I am not afraid of men."

"I'm not—" Angela stopped herself and went into the house.

Katy Brennan sat down on the top step. Now that Clint Adams was around, it might pay to stay around here a little while longer; but once Clint moved on, Katy was going to move out on her own as well.

In the bed that they shared, Bonnie Franks and Irene Dennison heard every word that passed between Angela and Katy.

"What do you think?" Bonnie asked.

"I think Katy's going to be leaving pretty soon."

"I hope not."

"Oh, she'll leave," Irene said. "She and Mother never did get along. I don't know how Mother ever talked Katy into coming along."

"We need Katy," Bonnie said. "She's strong."

"Mother is strong."

"Maybe that's why they don't get along."

"You girls had better get to sleep," Alice Williams whispered to them. "We have a lot of work to do tomorrow."

"Sure, Alice," Bonnie said.

"Yes, Alice," Irene said.

In the bed that she shared with Katy Brennan—
they were only able to afford three beds after they'd
bought the ranch—Alice Williams rolled over, plain-
ly worried. She had known from the beginning,
when they had first left New Jersey, that there
would be trouble between Angela Dennison and
Katy Brennan. They were the two strongest-willed
women she knew, and they would never be able to
get along. If Katy didn't leave soon, there was going
to be an explosion, one that none of them might
survive.

Sandra Ward moved over to make room in the bed
she shared with Angela Dennison.

"So?" she said.

"So what?" Angela asked, sitting on the bed.

"Did she?"

"Did she what?"

"Don't you play games with me, Angela," Sandra
said. "Did she sleep with him?"

"I'm sure she did," Angela said.

"Then she broke the agreement."

"Yes," Angela said, lying down.

"Angela—"

"I want to go to sleep now, Sandy."

"Sure," Sandra said. "You go to sleep."

Sandra rolled over onto her right side, away from
Angela. What was good for Katy, she thought, could
be good for her, too.

•   •   •

Angela was worried.

Now that Katy had broken their agreement, the others might start thinking that they could as well.

Even her own daughter, Irene.

If that happened, everything could come crashing down around them . . . again.

Chapter Eleven

When Clint first heard the noise in the house, he thought that it was Katy coming back.

Then he thought better of it: If Katy were going to come back, she never would have left.

He got out of bed, slipped on his pants, and picked up his gun from the night table.

He moved to the door, opened it a crack, and peered out. It was dark in the hall, but it was just as dark in the bedroom, and Clint had his night vision. He was able to see that the hall was empty, and he slipped out into the hall and moved toward the stairway.

When he reached the head of the steps, he stopped and listened. Again, he heard a sound—somebody bumping into something. It wasn't very loud, but it was loud enough.

In fact, in one respect, it was too loud.

There was someone in the house, and they were taking pains to make just enough noise to draw him out.

Somebody *wanted* him to go down the stairs.

He backed away from the steps, trying to figure out another way to get downstairs. There were no back stairs, so the only way for him to get from the second floor to the first floor without using the stairs was by way of a window.

He went back to his room and, sticking his gun into the front of his pants, opened the window. He grabbed the sheet from the bed and pulled it off, then tied one end to the foot of the bed. When he tossed the other end of the sheet out the window there was only a couple of feet dangling, but a couple of feet was all he needed to reduce the possibility of injuring himself when he dropped to the ground below.

Clint sat on the windowsill, swung his legs outside, grabbed hold of the sheet, and then lowered himself until he was hanging out the window. He looked below once and then released his hold on the sheet. For a moment he was suspended in the air, and then he landed, bending his knees to absorb the impact. He flexed his legs once to be sure he hadn't hurt himself, and then he moved around to the side of the house.

He knew for a fact that all of the windows had been locked, but the only way someone could have gotten into the house was to have forced one. In order for him to get back into the house without making any noise, he had to find that same window.

He checked one side of the house, and when he didn't find the window there, he moved around the back of the house again to the other side. He hoped that whoever was inside the house would not become impatient.

On this side of the house he finally found the forced

window. The wood had been splintered somehow, and it must have been the noise of it that had first awakened him.

As quietly as he could, he lifted himself up onto the sill and entered the house. Once inside, he crouched down and drew his gun. He found that he was in Beverly's office. He quietly moved to the door.

He waited now for the intruder to make some kind of sound to announce his location. It was now a matter of which of them had more patience.

Clint had almost reached the end of his when he finally heard it. It sounded like someone bumping into a piece of furniture.

The intruder was in the parlor.

From the parlor, the man would be able to flatten himself against the wall and watch the stairs. Fortunately for Clint, he was already downstairs. In fact, as he stepped from Beverly's office, his back was to the same wall that the intruder would be using for cover.

Clint moved slowly down the hall, hoping that the floorboards would not creak beneath his feet. If he could move along the wall until he was right next to the parlor entrance, he should be able to surprise the intruder and take him without firing his gun.

He was mentally counting the distance between himself and the doorway.

Five feet.

Four.

Three.

He could see the barrel of the intruder's gun sticking out from the doorway.

Two feet.

Then, as he had feared, a floorboard groaned loudly beneath his weight.

Things happened very quickly then. The intruder stepped out into the hall and fired his gun. His shot went wild, but the muzzle flash momentarily blinded Clint. Clint dropped to his knees as the intruder fired again, and he did the only thing he could. He fired his gun, and then he fired it again in the direction he'd last seen the man. He fired a third time and heard a shout of pain, and he pulled the trigger two more times. He could actually hear the bullets slap home, but just to be on the safe side, he flattened himself against the opposite wall. He had not fired the sixth bullet; even in the heat of the moment, he had preserved that round in case he needed it.

He had only been blinded for a matter of moments, and now that his sight had returned, he saw the man lying on the floor. Clint wasn't going to need the one round he had saved.

He moved to the body, and once he'd made sure the man was dead, he went to a nearby lamp and lit it. At that moment someone started banging on the front door. When he opened it, he saw Pevy and several other men standing on the porch with their guns in their hands.

"What's going on, Adams?" Pevy demanded.

"Send someone for the sheriff, Pevy," Clint said. "I've killed an intruder."

Chapter Twelve

They decided not to send for the sheriff.

Pevy had three men take the body out to the barn and wrap it in a blanket. In the morning, Clint would ride into town with Pevy, and the body.

After the men had left with the body, Clint and Pevy were alone in the house together.

"I knew you were trouble," Pevy said.

"It's my fault that someone broke into the house and tried to kill me?"

"If you weren't here, it wouldn't have happened."

Clint stared at the man. "You know what bothers me? I don't have an argument for that. I need a drink. Do you want one?"

Pevy looked surprised by the offer. "Yeah, sure."

"Let's go into Beverly's office."

They entered the office, and while Clint poured two glasses of expensive whiskey, Pevy looked at the damaged window.

"I'll have that fixed in the morning."

"Fine," Clint said, handing the man his drink.

Clint was careful not to sit behind Beverly's desk while Pevy was there. He didn't want to give the man something else to complain about. He walked over to a small divan that was in the room and sat on it. Pevy remained standing.

"Maybe he was a sneak thief," Pevy said suddenly. "Maybe he wasn't after you."

"He was after me."

"How can you be so sure?"

"I recognized him," Clint said.

He told Pevy about the run-in he'd had in town with the two men who were bothering Katy and Bonnie.

"He was one of the men?"

"The one I fought with," Clint said. "I have a feeling I'm being set up for something."

"You mean that since you had a fight with the man, now that he's dead, you'll be accused of killing him?"

"Well, I *did* kill him," Clint said, "but yeah, that's what I mean. I may be accused of deliberately killing him, and I have no witnesses to what really happened."

"Well, you have us," Pevy said, meaning he and his men. "I mean, we heard the shots. It's obvious that he broke in. Just look at the window."

"I could have done that afterward, to make it look like he broke in."

"Then what was he doing here?"

"There'd be a lot of questions, Pevy," Clint said, "but the fact remains I killed him, and it was only him and me in the house."

After a moment of silence, Pevy said, "No, it wasn't."

"What do you mean?"

"I mean there was five of us here."

"What?"

"We were playing poker," Pevy said, warming to his subject. "Don't you remember? There was you, me, Anderson, Killy and . . . Roseman. Yeah, we were playing poker, and you heard a noise and you . . . no, you and *me* went to take a look—"

"That won't work, Pevy," Clint said. "I mean, I appreciate it—"

"Why won't it work?"

"That'd be perjury. I can't ask you or any of your men to perjure yourselves."

"With us as witnesses," Pevy said, "it will never get that far."

"You have a point there," Clint said. He looked at the foreman. "I appreciate this, Pevy."

"Forget it," Pevy said abruptly. "I'm doing it for Miz Press. If she found out I let you get into trouble and didn't help you out of it, she'd fire me."

"No, she wouldn't."

"Yeah," Pevy said, "she would."

Clint stood up and walked over to the sidebar.

"Want another drink?"

Pevy thought a moment. "Sure, why not?"

Clint refilled the glasses and handed Pevy his.

"Will your men go along with it?"

"Sure," Pevy said. "They'll do whatever I tell them."

"I don't think we'll need any of them tomorrow. The two of us can take the body in and tell the sheriff the story. Do you know the sheriff?"

"We ain't friends, but I know him," Pevy said. "He

was elected a couple of months ago."

"How is he?"

"Too soon to say," Pevy said. "His name's Ransom, Daniel Ransom. He's young, about thirty-one or something."

"Experienced?"

"He was a deputy for a while here, and when old Tim Stoddard decided not to run again, Ransom ran and won."

"All right, so we'll see Ransom tomorrow."

"And then what?"

"What do you mean?"

"Will you be staying around?"

"Somebody tried to kill me, Pevy," Clint said, swirling the liquor in his glass. "What do you think?"

"Great," Pevy said, half to himself. "More trouble."

Yeah, Clint thought, but not for me.

Chapter Thirteen

In the morning they tied the body of the man Clint knew only as "Frank" to a horse and rode into town, trailing him behind them.

Pevy led the way to the sheriff's office, where they dismounted.

"Let me do the talking," Clint said. "If you don't *have* to say anything, it might be better."

"All right."

They went into the office and found the sheriff sitting at his desk, going over some posters. The man looked up at them and frowned.

"Pevy, isn't it?" he asked. "Foreman out at the Press ranch?"

"That's right," Pevy said.

"And you're Clint Adams," Sheriff Ransom said, "the Gunsmith, uh . . . *guest* out at the ranch."

"Right again."

"What can I do for you gentlemen?" he asked, sitting back.

"We've got a body on a horse outside."

"Whose?"

"I think his name is Frank something," Clint said. "That ring a bell?"

Ransom thought a moment and then said, "I can't say that it does."

Clint explained the altercation he'd had with the dead man and his friend and then went on to explain what had happened at the house the night before.

"I suppose the women involved will verify your story," Ransom said.

"I'm sure they will."

Ransom looked at Pevy. "And you'll back his story about last night?"

"Yes."

Ransom shrugged. "I don't see any problems then," he said, leaning forward and picking up a poster to examine it. "Why don't you take the body over to the undertaker's?"

"That's it?" Clint asked.

"I'll check on it later, Mr. Adams."

"On the body?" Clint asked. "Why, it's not going anywhere. Why don't you check with his friend and see what he was doing sneaking up on me last night?"

"Obviously, he didn't like the outcome of your fight," Ransom said. "What other reason could he have had?"

"I don't know," Clint said, "but I'd sure like to find out."

"Then why don't you ask his friend?"

"You're the law."

"And you're the Gunsmith," Ransom said. "That sounds like enough of a reason for someone to try and kill you, to me. I'm sure it's happened to you before."

"Too many times."

"That's the price you pay for carrying a rep around with you."

"I don't need a lecture from a young—"

"All right, Sheriff," Pevy said, cutting Clint off. "Thanks for your time. We'll be going now."

Clint wasn't quite through, but Pevy tugged him toward the door.

When they were outside, Clint said, "That's supposed to be a lawman?"

"Must be a new breed," Pevy said. "Come on, let's take the body over to the undertaker, and then you can find this feller's friend and question him."

"If I can find him," Clint said. "When he finds out what happened to his friend, he may not want to talk to me."

"I wouldn't blame him."

As they walked the body over to the undertaker, Clint asked, "What do you know about your neighbor, Tom Kennedy?"

"Came into the area just after I did; started buying up as much land as he could get."

"Did he make Beverly an offer?"

"Several, but she wasn't selling."

"How did he take it?"

"He's a businessman," Pevy said. "How should he take it? Wait a minute: Are you thinking Kennedy had something to do with this?"

"He came to the house last night."

"What for?"

"I don't know," Clint said. "I think he just wanted to see who I was."

"And when he did, he sent this feller after you?"

"Possibly."

"Why?"

"Because he wants the land those women are on, and he thinks I'm working for them."

"Why would he think that? Oh, I see: because you came to their defense."

"Exactly."

"Well," Pevy said, scratching his neck, "I don't know Kennedy well enough to say. I guess you're going to have to talk to him about that yourself."

"I guess I am," Clint said.

After Clint and Pevy had left his office, Sheriff Ransom got up and moved to his window, to make sure they were walking toward the undertaker's office. When they were out of sight, he left his office and rushed over to the saloon. It wasn't open yet, but he knew he'd find Sammy Judd out in front, waiting.

Judd was there, all right, asleep against the horse trough.

"Sammy, wake up!" Ransom said, shaking the man with his foot.

When that failed to wake him, the sheriff leaned over, took Judd's hat off, filled it with water from the trough, and poured it over the man's head.

Judd came to life, sputtering and shouting something about drowning.

"What a dream!" Judd said, spitting out water.

"Are you awake, Sammy?"

"Sure, sure," Judd said, squinting at the sheriff. "I'm awake."

"You know who I am?"

Judd squinted again. "The sheriff?"

"That's right, the sheriff," Ransom said. "Listen to me now, Judd, and listen good."

"I'm listening," the disheveled town drunk said.

"Go over to the livery and tell Bart Kincaid to give you a horse. Tell him to charge it to me, all right?"

"Sure, but what am I gonna do with a horse?"

"You ride out to Tom Kennedy's ranch and tell Kennedy that Clint Adams just brought in his man, Frank Lobo, dead. Do you understand?"

"Sure, Sheriff," Judd said, nodding. "I understand. Frank Lobo's dead."

"Tell Mr. Kennedy that Adams will probably be out to see him, and he is probably looking for Teddy Rigg right now. You got all that?"

"Yeah, I got it," Judd said. "Teddy Rigg. I got it, Sheriff."

"Get goin'."

"Get goin'," Judd repeated, nodding, "right." He turned to go, but then turned back. "Uh, Sheriff?"

"What?"

"I, uh, won't be here when the saloon opens."

"When you get back the saloon will be here," the sheriff assured him.

"Yeah, but I'll miss about an hour—"

"There'll be a couple of drinks waiting for you, Sammy—on the house."

Judd brightened immediately. "On the house?"

"And on me, Sammy," the sheriff said. "Now get goin'."

"I'm goin'," Judd said, stumbling away. "I'm gone."

After leaving the body at the undertaker's, Clint and Pevy separated outside the office.

"I have to see about repairing that busted window," Pevy said.

"I'll look around town and see if I can find either Kennedy or the other man—uh, Teddy," Clint said. "I don't know his full name, but maybe someone will recognize him by his first name and description."

"I'll see you back at the ranch then?"

"Yeah," Clint said, "back at the ranch."

"Good luck."

"Thanks."

Pevy nodded and started off.

"Pevy?"

"Yeah?"

"I think it would be a good idea to set up a watch at the ranch—just in case."

Pevy thought a moment, then nodded shortly and said, "I think you're right."

"Pevy," Clint said, "if we're not careful, we might become friends."

"Bite your tongue," Pevy said, and he moved on.

Chapter Fourteen

Sammy Judd couldn't get in to see Tom Kennedy until he invoked the name of the sheriff.

"Wait here," Del Beman, one of Kennedy's men, said. "I'll check with the boss."

"Go ahead and check," Judd said, anxious to get back to town and those free drinks.

Beman went inside and returned moments later.

"Come on, Sammy."

Sammy Judd followed Beman through the house to Kennedy's office, where he relayed the sheriff's message. All the while, Judd was staring at the drink decanters on Kennedy's wall.

"All right, Sammy," Kennedy said. "Tell the sheriff I thank him for his message."

"I'll tell him, sir," Judd said, licking his lips as he stared at the amber, red, and brown liquids in the various decanters.

Kennedy saw where the man was looking and

smiled. "Would you like a drink before you start back, Sammy?" he asked.

"Well, sir," Judd said, touching his dry lower lip with his fingers, "maybe just one."

"Of course," Kennedy said, walking to the bar. "Whiskey, or brandy?"

Judd's eyes brightened as he asked, "Uh, is it good brandy?"

"The best."

"A brandy, then," Judd said, straightening to his full height.

"You know good brandy, Sammy?" Kennedy asked, handing him the brandy snifter.

"Mr. Kennedy," Sammy Judd said, "I am an authority on all liquors."

"I'm sure you are, Sammy," Kennedy said. He shook his head as Judd tossed back the brandy as if it were a shot of whiskey.

"Ahhh," Judd said, smacking his lips.

Kennedy turned to Beman. "Show him out and then come back. Find Teddy Rigg. And bring Walt Denver with you."

"Sure, boss."

Kennedy sat down behind his desk and waited for his men to return. He wanted to ask Rigg what Frank Lobo was doing getting killed by Clint Adams.

Moments later three men entered the office. Kennedy motioned Rigg closer to his desk, while Beman and Denver stood to either side of the door.

"I just heard that Clint Adams killed Frank Lobo last night."

Rigg swallowed hard.

"How did that happen, Rigg?"

"I don't know, Mr. Kennedy," Rigg said. "I wasn't there."

"Wasn't where?"

"At the Press ranch?"

"Is that where it happened?"

Rigg swallowed again. "I dunno," he said. "I just figured—"

"No, Rigg," Kennedy said, "you did more than figure. You sent Lobo to the Press ranch to kill Clint Adams, didn't you?"

"Uh . . ."

"Don't deny it," Kennedy said, sitting back in his chair. "I hired you, and you brought Lobo along. He was your man. He did what you told him."

"I was just trying to help you, Mr. Kennedy," Rigg said finally.

"By implicating me in an attempted murder?" Kennedy asked. "Did you really think that Lobo could kill Clint Adams?"

Rigg was speechless. He just didn't have the skills to defend himself against Kennedy's onslaught.

"I think you've worked for me long enough, Rigg," Kennedy said.

"Mr. Kennedy—"

"Clint Adams is looking for you," Kennedy said. "He wants to ask you some questions."

"I wouldn't tell him nothin', Mr. Kennedy."

"I know you won't, Rigg," Kennedy said, "because you're leaving. Here."

Kennedy took out some money and tossed the bills across the desk at Rigg. They struck the man on the chest and fluttered to the floor. Rigg bent over to retrieve them.

"What's this for?"

"Severance pay."

"What?"

"You're fired, Rigg."

"Now, Mr. Kennedy—"

"Boys," Kennedy said to the men standing at the door, "show Mr. Rigg off my land. And make sure he rides *away* from town."

"This way, Rigg," Beman said.

"Mr. Kennedy—"

"This way!" Beman said again, tugging on Rigg's arm.

As Rigg turned and walked to the door, Beman looked at Kennedy, who nodded. Beman and Denver had worked for Kennedy longer than anyone else, and Beman understood what he was supposed to do.

"Del?"

"Yes, sir?"

"When you're done," Kennedy said, "go to town and send that telegram we talked about."

"Yes, sir."

"Good-bye, Rigg," Kennedy said.

Rigg turned his head to look at Kennedy, then looked at Beman and Denver as they escorted him out of the office.

Kennedy thought from the look on his face that Rigg knew what was coming.

Chapter Fifteen

Clint couldn't find "Teddy," and no one admitted to knowing him when Clint described him. It was obvious that Clint was going to have to ride out to Tom Kennedy's ranch and return the visit from the night before. Maybe he'd find Teddy out there.

On his way to the livery, he noticed the sheriff walking toward him. The man's head was down, though, and it was obvious that he hadn't noticed Clint.

"Hello, Sheriff," Clint said as they converged.

"Huh?" Sheriff Ransom jerked his head up and seemed startled when he saw Clint standing there. "Oh, uh, Adams."

"Have you been to the undertaker's yet?" Clint asked.

"Uh, no, not yet. I haven't had time."

"Been busy, huh?"

"Yes, I've been busy," Ransom said.

The man seemed nervous to Clint—too nervous

for a man who had *not* seemed intimidated earlier, when they were in his office. That meant it wasn't Clint's reputation that was making the man nervous but probably something he had done between then and now.

"Well, you'd better get over there before the feller's personal belongings disappear."

"Sure, I'll do that," Ransom said.

"Everything all right, Sheriff?"

"Uh, sure, why do you ask?"

"You just seem . . . edgy, that's all," Clint said.

"I have to go, Adams," Ransom said, brusquely. "I have things to do."

"Sure, Sheriff, sure," Clint said. "I have things to do, too."

The sheriff nodded jerkily and started off again. Clint stared after the man, whose shoulders were hunched as if he were expecting a blow. Or a bullet.

A rich man like Tom Kennedy probably had his spies in town, and Ransom wouldn't be the first sheriff who was sitting in a rich man's pocket.

It seemed likely that Ransom had probably sent Kennedy word that one of his men was dead and that Clint Adams was on his way to see him.

Well, that was fine. It would give Kennedy time to think about what he'd say. The lie would be so elaborate that it would be obvious, even to Kennedy.

When Del Beman and Walt Denver rode into town, they saw Clint Adams talking to Sheriff Ransom. From the way the sheriff scooted away, it was clear that he was skittish—to say the least.

"What do you think?" Beman asked Denver.

"We'd better keep an eye on him," Denver said. "I never did think he had the stomach for the job."

"Neither did I," Beman said. He watched as Clint Adams crossed the street. "I wonder if I'd have the stomach to face the Gunsmith."

Denver looked at Beman. "I guess we're lucky that we don't have to find out. That'd be Trey Hatcher's job."

"Right," Beman said. "Let's get that telegraph message sent."

"It's gonna be somethin' to see," Walt Denver said. "Trey Hatcher against the Gunsmith."

"Adams is old," Beman said, "and Hatcher's young. I'll put my money on Hatcher."

Denver looked at Beman and asked, "How much?"

"Huh?"

"How much money you willing to bet?"

"I didn't mean—"

"Chickening out now, huh?"

"I ain't," Beman said, frowning. "All right, I'll bet you ten dollars."

"Ten!" Denver said derisively. "What about fifty?"

"Fifty dollars?"

"Fifty dollars says Adams can take Trey Hatcher," Denver said. "Is it a bet?"

Beman thought it over. "It's a bet. Now let's get that telegram sent."

Clint stopped on the other side of the street and watched the two men ride past. He had seen them watching him and wondered if they were Tom Kennedy's men. He looked quickly and caught the brand on one of the horses. It didn't take a genius to figure out that "TK" was Tom Kennedy's brand.

If they were going to watch him, he decided to watch them for a while, too.

Chapter Sixteen

Clint watched the men as they tied off their horses in front of the telegraph office. He found a straight-backed wooden chair in front of the general store and sat in it.

They were in the office long enough to send a telegram, and when they came out they stopped on the boardwalk and stared at Clint. Clint had had no previous intention to confront the men, but he found himself standing up and crossing the street toward them.

"Walt," Beman said.

"Stand fast, Del," Denver said. "He could kill us both, but he won't if we don't give him a reason to."

"Guess I know the answer to my question now."

"What question?"

"About whether or not I'd have the stomach to face the Gunsmith."

Walt Denver swallowed hard. "Yeah, me too."

• • •

Clint saw the two men talking to each other, but their stances said that they had no intention of doing anything but wait for him to reach them.

"Hello, boys."

"Adams."

"Good," Clint said, "then we don't have to pretend you don't know who I am, and we don't have to pretend that I don't know who you work for."

"So?" said Denver. "What's next?"

That stopped Clint. He didn't know what was next, because he hadn't thought it out.

"You boys send a telegram for your boss?"

"What if we did?" Denver said. "It's none of your business."

"You may be right," Clint said. "Then again, you may not be."

"What's that mean?"

"Seems to me your boss is worried about something," Clint said. "Maybe he thinks he needs more help than he's got now."

"My boss don't worry about nothin'," Beman said.

"Is that a fact?" Clint said. "I'd send him a message that I'm coming out to see him, but my guess is he already knows that. Maybe that's why he sent you two in to send a telegram."

"We got no reason to talk to you, Adams," Denver said.

"If that's true, then why don't you walk?" Clint asked him.

Denver looked over at Beman, who returned the glance. It was Denver who nodded, and then both men began to walk off tentatively.

Clint didn't know what he had accomplished by

that. He decided that the only way he *was* going to accomplish anything would be to go out and talk to Tom Kennedy himself.

He started away, then stopped, looked at the telegraph office, and finally went inside.

Denver and Beman saw Clint Adams walk into the telegraph office.

"Do you think he'll find out who we sent the message to?" Beman asked.

"Why not?" Denver said. "All he has to do is show the clerk two bits."

"So what should we—"

"Shh."

They watched as Clint came out and walked to the livery. Several minutes later, he came riding out on his horse and left town.

"Do you think he's headin' for the ranch?" Del Beman asked.

"What do you think?" Denver grabbed his partner's arm and said, "Come on. We can get there ahead of him. He'll follow the road."

"We gonna bushwhack him?"

Denver scowled at Beman. "You remember what happened to the last feller who made that decision?"

"How could I forget?" Beman said.

"Come on," Denver said. "We'll be there in case the boss needs us."

Clint knew there was a possibility that the two men would follow him. After all, hadn't one of Kennedy's men tried to kill him the night before? Still, he didn't think they would. Further, he didn't think Kennedy had really known anything about the attempt. It had been a foolish move, and he didn't think Tom Kennedy was a foolish man. He'd be a lot more deliberate than that.

He'd send for a gunman named Trey Hatcher.

Chapter Seventeen

Clint had heard of Trey Hatcher. He was a young man who had made a name for himself lately—"lately" being the past three or four years.

Hatcher had killed ten men in four years, including Johnny Abel and Dominick Lutz, both of whom had reputations of their own. Of course, Hatcher's real claim to fame was the fact that he had killed the Haywood brothers—Gar, Les, and Percy. The Haywoods had had a reputation for turning the tide in range wars by virtue of their presence. In this particular instance, however, the other side had hired Trey Hatcher, and the rest was the stuff that penny dreadfuls were made of.

Trey Hatcher's reputation had soared after that.

Now he was on his way to Little Creek, Wyoming, to try his luck against the reputation of the Gunsmith.

That was an opportunity men like Trey Hatcher waited most of their lives for.

To Clint Adams, Hatcher was just another in a long line of reputation seekers.

Trey Hatcher read the telegram again, then leaned over the girl lying next to him to place the slip on the night table.

"What's that about?" she asked.

He trailed his hand across her large breasts, flicking the nipples with his forefinger.

"Just a job, sweetheart," Hatcher lied. It was more than that to him, he thought, as he slid his hand down over her belly and into the tangle of hair below. "Like what I am to you."

"Ooh," she said as he dipped his finger into her, "you're more than a job, Trey. You know that."

"That's all right," he said, moving his finger around inside of her. He liked the way she was becoming juicy. "You do your job well, honey, and that's all I care about."

"You do your job well too, Trey, don't you?" she asked. She bit her lip and lifted her hips off the bed as he put more fingers to work on her.

"I do my job very well," Trey Hatcher said, sliding one leg over her and mounting her. "But it's never paid off the way it's going to pay off in Little Creek, Wyoming."

This was a helluva lot more than a job to Trey Hatcher.

This was his chance to really make his reputation and a big chunk of money, both at the same time.

The Gunsmith, he thought as he drove himself into the whore. Just thinking about killing the Gunsmith had given him an erection so hard he thought it would never go down.

Now he'd find out just how good she really was at her job.

Chapter Eighteen

As Clint approached Tom Kennedy's ranch, he was impressed. The house, the barn, the corral—all were just a little larger than Beverly's. There were a bunch of men around the corral, and they all turned and looked his way as he rode by.

As he approached the house, a man came trotting over from the corral and stopped when he reached the steps.

"Can I help ya?" He was a solid man of medium height, in his forties, and he favored his right leg a bit, as if he had an old injury.

"I'm here to see Mr. Kennedy."

"What's your business?"

"He'll know," Clint said. "Just tell him Clint Adams is here to see him, will you?"

"Wait a minute," the man said. He turned away, but then he turned back and said, "That's a beautiful animal you're riding."

"Thanks."

"Wait here a minute."

The man limped up the steps and went into the house. When he came out, he was accompanied by Tom Kennedy.

"Come on in, Mr. Adams," Kennedy said. "I guess we have some talking to do."

"I guess so," Clint said, dismounting.

"Eddie will take care of your horse for you." The gimpy man came down the steps, favoring his right leg even more.

"It'll be a pleasure," Eddie said.

Clint handed the man the reins, noticing that he had scarred hands and was missing a finger on the left.

"Been handling horses for a long time, have you?" he asked the man.

"Most of my life," Eddie said. "Got this from a horse," he added, slapping his injured leg.

"Mr. Adams?" Kennedy said impatiently.

"Take good care of him," Clint said.

"Count on it."

Clint mounted the steps and walked past Kennedy into the house.

"This way," Kennedy said, passing him now. "We can talk in my office."

Clint followed Kennedy to his office, where the man seated himself behind his desk.

"A drink?" Kennedy asked.

"A little early," Clint said. "Tell me, what is it you think we have to talk about?"

Kennedy took a moment to light a long, thin, black cigar.

"How much do you want?" he finally asked.

"To do what?"

"To leave Little Creek," Kennedy said. "Or Wyoming, for that matter."

"And why would you want me to leave?" Clint asked.

"I don't want any trouble with you, Adams."

"That's not the impression I got last night."

"Look," Kennedy said, "I'll be honest with you. I know about last night, and I had nothing to do with it."

"I didn't think so."

"What?" Kennedy said, frowning.

"It was a stupid thing to do, Kennedy, and you don't strike me as a stupid man. At least you didn't, until just now."

"What do you mean?"

"What makes you think I could be bought?"

"Come on, Adams," Kennedy said. "A man of your reputation, a gun for hire, what else would you want?"

"You'd better check my reputation again, Kennedy," Clint said. "You'll find out that my gun has *never* been for hire. As for leaving Wyoming, I have no intention of doing that for a while. I still need to find the man who sent Frank Lobo after me."

"That would be Teddy Rigg."

"I only had a first name up until now, but yeah, it would be."

"Well then, you will be leaving Wyoming after all," Kennedy said.

"What makes you say that?"

"Well, Rigg has left, so I assume you'll be following him."

"He's left?"

"I fired him."

"Instead of turning him over to the law?"

"Why do that? He'd just deny that he had anything to do with Lobo's attempt on you. The law wouldn't be able to touch him."

"But you fired him?"

"I detest incompetence," Kennedy said, "and stupidity. As you said, Adams, I am not a stupid man, and I will not have stupid men working for me."

"So you fired him because Lobo missed?"

"Adams," Kennedy said, "I'll tell you again, I don't want you dead."

"That's why you've sent for Trey Hatcher?"

Kennedy stopped his cigar halfway to his mouth. "Who told you that?"

"I found out about it," Clint said. "That's all you have to know."

"Well, as it happens, I sent for Hatcher for an entirely different reason."

"And what's that?"

"Self-defense."

"Against who?"

"Against you."

"That's a different reason?"

"I didn't send for him to kill you," Kennedy said, "but to protect me from you."

"And what makes you think you need protection from me?" Clint asked.

"Well, if you're working for those women—"

"What women?"

"I thought we were being frank here, Adams," Kennedy said. "Those six women who have squatted on my land."

"*Your* land?"

"Well, it would have been my land if they hadn't come along," he said. "There's water on that land that I need."

"So make a deal with them to let you use the water," Clint said. "I'm sure they'd be reasonable."

Kennedy scowled. It was plain that he did not see himself making a deal with six women for something that he already considered his.

"If they were going to be reasonable they would have taken one of my offers to buy the place."

"So you'd rather try to force them off than make a deal?"

"Let's just say I'd rather they leave."

"You're not admitting that you're trying to force them off?"

"In what way?"

"Well, by having your men harass them."

"I had nothing to do with that, either."

"I see," Clint said. "You'll simply hide behind the actions of your men."

Kennedy didn't answer.

Clint stood up.

"Are you working for those women?"

"No," Clint said, "but I won't stand by and watch you force them from their property."

"Then you see why I've sent for Trey Hatcher."

"Look, Kennedy," Clint said, "for whatever reason you may have hired him, keep your hired gun out of my way."

"Afraid of him?" Kennedy asked.

"I'm always afraid when I think I might have to kill a man," Clint said. "Tell that to your man Hatcher when he gets here."

•   •   •

After Clint Adams had left his office, Kennedy stood up, walked to another door, and opened it. Walt Denver and Del Beman stepped into the room.

"What do you think, Boss?" Beman asked.

"I think Trey Hatcher had better be as good as I've heard he is," Kennedy said.

"What about those women?" Denver asked.

Kennedy crushed out his cigar viciously and said, "Make their lives miserable. Starting today."

Chapter Nineteen

Clint rode from Kennedy's ranch back to Beverly Press's place.

"Is Pevy back?" he asked a man called Parkinson as he handed Duke over to him.

"Yes, sir," Parkinson said. "He got back a little while ago."

"Where is he?"

"I'm not sure," Parkinson said, "but I can check."

"That's okay," Clint said. "I'll find him. Thanks anyway."

Clint went into the house and stopped when he smelled something cooking. Mrs. Marshall must have come back and started lunch. He took a detour and walked to the kitchen. As he entered, though, he saw that it wasn't Mrs. Marshall at the stove at all, but a much younger woman with dark hair. As she turned to face him, he recognized her as one of the women who lived with Katy Brennan.

"Sandra Ward, right?" he asked.

She smiled, her white teeth contrasting sharply with the blackness of her hair.

"That's right," she said, "but you can call me Sandy. Are you hungry?"

"As it happens," Clint said, "I am, but how—"

"Go and wash up for lunch," she said. "We can talk later."

"But how—"

"Go," she said. "Lunch is almost ready."

Shaking his head, Clint left the kitchen and went upstairs to clean up—as he'd been instructed.

When he came back down, the table was set for two and Sandy was standing next to it, waiting for him.

"Good, you're here. Sit down and I'll serve lunch."

Clint took a seat and waited while she went back into the kitchen. She returned with a tray laden with meat, vegetables, and . . .

"Potato pancakes," she said, putting one on his plate. "My specialty. Try it."

He cut a piece off and tasted it.

"It's delicious," he said, really meaning it.

She added a small steak and some carrots to the plate, then said, "I'll go and get the biscuits."

By the time she returned he had tasted the meat and carrots and found everything delicious.

"I do all the cooking for the six of us," she said, seating herself.

"Won't they miss you for lunch?" he asked.

"I left lunch for them."

"Where do they think you are?"

She shrugged. "Out."

She poured each of them a glass of wine. "Now, isn't this nice?"

"It's very nice, Sandy," he said, "really, but I'm curious."

"About what?"

"About what you're doing here," he said. "And how you got in."

"There was a broken window on the side of the house when I got here," she said. "I climbed in."

"That was supposed to be fixed."

"It has been," she said. "But I was already inside by then."

"Why?"

"I . . . wanted to talk to you. When I saw the kitchen—it's a beautiful kitchen—I just got carried away. I hope you don't mind."

"I don't mind," Clint said, "but Mrs. Marshall might be a bit peeved."

"Who is she?"

"The cook."

"Why isn't she here?"

"I gave her some time off."

"Then you needed someone to cook for you," Sandy said. "I'm glad I came."

"Sandy," he said, "did Katy, uh, say anything—I mean—did she—"

"Did she tell me that she slept with you? No, but we all guessed it. She had an argument with Angela when she got back last night."

"I see."

"She broke our agreement."

"I'm sorry—"

"Don't be," Sandy said. "I'm glad she broke it.

We all figured she'd be the first to do it."

"You expected it?"

"Sure, and a lot sooner than this."

"And you don't mind?"

"Well, Angela's pretty upset about it. She thinks that the rest of us are going to break it now."

"And are you?"

Sandra Ward smiled. "Why do you think I'm here, silly?"

Sandy Ward was insatiable in bed.

After lunch she said she'd take care of the dishes later and practically dragged him up to his room, where she quickly disrobed and threw herself on him.

She was taller and more slender than Katy, but her breasts, though smaller, were firm, and she was as skillful at lovemaking as Katy had been.

Clint felt that he was extending himself in order to satisfy her. He made a concerted effort to hold back until he knew she was ready, and then both went over the edge together.

"Whoa," she said, lying on her back.

He agreed.

"This makes me wish *I'd* been the first to break the agreement."

"I'm flattered."

"I have to catch my breath before I take care of the dishes."

"Take your time," he said, out of breath himself. "Tell me something."

"What?"

"If Angela is the only one who really wanted the agreement, why did you all agree?"

"Angela has a strong personality," Sandy said. "I think she just . . . drove it into us. Maybe she even made us think we wanted it, too, but later we all agreed that she was the only one who *really* hated men."

"Does that include her daughter?"

"Little Irene? She *loves* men, but she's afraid of her mother." Clint, still catching his breath, heaved a sigh of relief. He didn't know what he'd do if Irene showed up. She was so young he might not be able to keep up with her. And he might give himself a heart attack trying.

"I guess we're all a little afraid of Angela," Sandy continued. "Or we were, before we came out here."

"Why is it different out here?"

"I don't know," she said. "Maybe it's the wild, untamed quality of the West that makes us all feel different."

"Except for Angela."

"I guess."

Her hand rested lightly on Clint's belly and began to inch lower.

"Sandy . . ."

"The dishes can wait," she said, her voice husky. "I can't."

"Sandy . . ."

Her hand touched his shriveled penis, stroking it, coaxing it half-erect.

"I know what you need," she said.

Before he could say anything she was between his legs, and her tongue and lips were avidly working on him. In a matter of seconds she had him hard, and she took him into her talented mouth.

Chapter Twenty

Clint left Sandy asleep and went downstairs to clear the dishes from the table. There was something nagging at the back of his mind about both Katy Brennan and Sandy Ward, but he couldn't quite bring it into the light where he could examine it.

When all of the dishes were stowed in the kitchen, he went outside to look for Pevy. The foreman was in front of the bunkhouse, talking to three of his men.

"There you are," Pevy said when Clint approached.

"I've been looking for you, too."

"These men are taking the first watch," Pevy said. "Do you have anything to say to them?"

"No," Clint said. "Just keep your eyes open, that's all."

"For what?" one of them asked.

"Anything that shouldn't be," Clint said.

"All right, go on," Pevy said. "Take your positions."

As the men left, Pevy moved closer to Clint. "How was your afternoon?"

For a moment Clint wondered if Pevy knew about Sandy, but he decided that he didn't. He was asking about Clint's search.

"I had a talk with Kennedy."

"And?"

"He says he had nothing to do with Frank Lobo trying to kill me. He also says that he fired Teddy Rigg."

"The other man?"

Clint nodded.

"You think he fired him or had him killed?"

Clint was surprised that he himself had not suspected such a thing.

"Now that you mention it," he said, "he did say that Rigg had left Wyoming."

"Yeah," Pevy said, "the hard way."

"You know of a man named Hatcher?"

"Trey Hatcher?" Pevy asked.

"That's the one."

"Does he work for Kennedy?"

"He does now," Clint said. "Kennedy sent for him today."

"Where's he coming from?"

"Three days away," Clint said.

"Great," Pevy said. "What do we do when he gets here?"

"We don't do anything, Pevy," Clint said.

"What do you mean?"

"I'm going to move to the hotel in town."

"Why?"

"Because that will take you, your men, and the ranch out of the picture."

"And leave you in the picture all by yourself!"

"That's the way it should be," Clint said. "It's my problem, after all."

"That ain't the way it started," Pevy said. "Seems to me it's them women who had the problem first, and you dealt yourself in."

"And see what it got me?"

"So now I'm dealing myself in," Pevy said.

"And your men? And the welfare of this ranch? How would Beverly feel about that?"

"She'd do the same thing."

"Pevy," Clint said, "you're the foreman of this ranch. It's your job to think of the welfare of this place above everything else. Can you deny that?"

"Well, no," Pevy said, reluctantly, "but—"

"No *buts*," Clint said. "I'll move my gear tomorrow morning, and you'll be out of it."

"Well," Pevy said, "my men and the ranch will be out of it."

"Meaning?"

"Meaning I've got the taste of this thing in my mouth and I don't like it. The only way for me to get rid of it is to see it through."

"Pevy . . ."

"Yeah?"

Clint hesitated, then said something entirely different from what he had been going to say: "You got a first name?"

"Sure I do."

"What is it?"

"I'd rather not say."

"Look," Clint said, "if you're going to get killed because of me, the least you can do is tell me your full name."

"Well . . ." Pevy said, "why not? You'll have to get it right on the headstone."

Clint waited. Pevy took some time and then finally spoke.

"It's Algernon."

"What?"

Pevy frowned. "Algernon." His tone dared Clint to make something of it.

"Algernon," Clint repeated.

"Yeah."

"That's it?"

"No," Pevy said. "It's Algernon Preston Pevy."

"Algernon Preston Pevy," Clint repeated.

"That's it."

Clint stared at Pevy for a few moments, then said, "That's going to have to be a big headstone."

"Just put Al Pevy," Pevy said. "It will save you money."

Clint smiled. "You got a deal."

"If I'm in this thing," Pevy said, "you better tell me *exactly* what the hell I'll be getting killed for."

Clint took a quick glance at the house, then looked at Pevy and said, "Women."

Pevy thought that over. "I can think of worse things to die for."

When Clint returned to the house, Sandy was coming out of the kitchen, drying her hands on a towel.

"Dishes are all cleaned and put away," Sandy said. "I don't think your Mrs. Marshall will ever be able to tell I was here."

"I wouldn't bet on it."

She tossed aside the towel, reached for him, and kissed him. Her tongue moved slowly in and out of his mouth, and she moaned and pressed herself against him.

"I have to go," she said, her tone clearly stating that she would rather stay.

"I understand."

"Well," she said, moving away from him, "now you've had Katy *and* me."

"You're not going to ask me who was better, are you?" he asked hopefully.

"Of course not," she said. "I wouldn't do that."

"Good."

"Besides, we're pretty close."

He had to agree with that. There wasn't very much to separate the two, and he'd have been hard put to pick one of them over the other.

"Wouldn't it be funny if we both came back here tonight?" she asked.

"It would be even funnier if you both came tomorrow," he said.

"Why?"

"Because as of tomorrow morning, I'll be at the hotel in town."

"Why?"

"When Kennedy and his men come for me, I don't want to cause this ranch any damage."

"You'll stand against them alone?"

"Well, there won't be many of them," he said. "Just the gunman he hired—at first, anyway."

"I've got a better idea," she said.

"What?"

"Come and stay with us."

"With you!" he said, shocked. "Angela would love that."

"I'll tell her you're there to protect us."

"The house is too small for the six of you," he said, "without trying to squeeze me in. She'd never go for that."

"Come back there with me now," she said. "If the others agree, she'll have to go along, too."

"Sandy," he said, "I don't know that this is a good idea."

"If Kennedy decides to really try and push us off, Clint, we're going to need help."

"Are you asking me to help?"

"We didn't have to ask you before," she said. "Do we have to now?"

"No," he said. "I'm in this already."

"Then you'll ride back with me and talk to Angela?"

He nodded and said, "Let's go."

Chapter Twenty-One

They saw the smoke before they came in view of the house.

"Oh, no!" Sandy cried. "Oh God!"

They urged their horses into a gallop, Clint and Duke leaving Sandy and her poor excuse for a horse behind. "This was all we could afford," she had said when Clint saw the nag she was riding.

When Clint rode in sight of the house, he saw that it was burning. There were five women standing outside, watching the flames.

As Clint approached them they turned, and, in spite of the situation, he saw Angela Dennison scowl.

"Clint!" Katy Brennan said as he dismounted.

"Are you all right?" he asked. "All of you?"

Katy rested her head on his chest and said, "We're fine. They made us get out of the house b-before they set f-fire to the place."

She lifted her head to look up when Sandy came riding up on them.

"Katy, honey, are you all right?" Sandy asked, dismounting.

"I'm fine," Katy said, backing away from Clint. She looked at Clint and Sandy critically. "Had to get in on the act, huh, Sandy?"

Sandy smiled. "Why not?"

Katy frowned, then brightened and shrugged. "Why not? Besides, we've got other problems, as you can see."

"Is everyone all right?" Sandy asked.

"We're fine," said Angela harshly. "It'll take more than this to force us off this land."

"How much more, Mother?" Irene Dennison asked.

Angela spun around to face her daughter. "A hell of a lot more, Irene!"

"Who was it?" Clint asked.

"Who do you think?" Angela said. "Kennedy."

"You saw him?"

"Of course we didn't see him," she said. "He wasn't here, but they were his men."

"Are you sure?"

"Who else could it be?"

"That's not being sure, Angela," Clint said.

"I saw the brand on the horses," Alice Williams said, stepping closer to them.

"What was it?" Clint asked.

"A *T* and a *K*," Alice answered.

"Are you sure?"

"Positive," she said. She touched her cheek, which was beginning to show a bruise. "I got a close look at the horse of the one who hit me."

"One of them hit you?" Clint asked. "With what?"

"Oh, he just backhanded me because I got too close

to his horse," the older woman said.

"Are you all right?" Clint asked. "Do you want to see a doctor?"

"No, I'm fine," Alice said. "I've been hit before."

"By men!" Angela said.

"And women," Alice said, giving Clint a smile. "I'm fine, thank you."

Clint turned to Katy and Sandy. "How many horses do you have?"

"We *had* three," said Sandy.

Clint looked around, but there were no horses in sight, except for his and Sandy's.

"They ran the horses off," Bonnie said.

"Small loss," Irene said. "They were nags."

"Like this one?" Clint asked, pointing to the horse Sandy had ridden.

"Worse than that one," Bonnie said.

"Well then, there's no use running them down," Clint said. "I'll ride back to the Press ranch and bring back some horses."

"What for?" Angela asked.

"So you and the other women can ride back to the ranch."

"And leave this place for Kennedy to take over?"

"No," Clint said. "I'll bring some men back and some lumber, and we'll build you a new house."

"Overnight?" Angela asked.

"Well, maybe not overnight—"

"Well, I'm not leaving here," Angela said.

"Mother . . ." Irene started.

"Angela, no . . ." said Alice.

"The rest of you can go," Angela said, "but I'm staying."

"Angela—" Katy started, but Clint put his hand on her arm, stopping her.

"Let's worry about that later," Clint said. "I'll go and get some horses. Any of you who wants to return to the Press house can use them."

"What if those men come back?" Irene asked.

"I don't think they will," Clint said. "They've done what they came to do."

"Still—" Irene began, but her mother cut her off.

"Oh, Irene, if you're worried, then ride back with Mr. Adams."

"On that nag?" Irene asked.

"You can ride double with me," Clint said. "This horse would only slow us down, and we can make better time on Duke, even riding double."

"All right," Irene said.

Clint mounted up, then reached down for Irene and hauled her up behind him.

"Hold on," he said.

She slid her arms around his waist and held on, pressing herself tightly against him.

Maybe too tightly.

"I should be back within a few hours," Clint said. "It will probably take a few hours more than that to get the lumber out here. We probably won't be able to start building until tomorrow."

"Then you'd better bring me a tent," Angela said, "because I'm staying."

"Oh, Mother!" Irene said, squeezing Clint's waist.

"See you soon," Clint said. "Oh, do you still have your guns?"

"They were in there," Angela said, indicating the burning house.

"Here," Clint said, handing his rifle down to her. "Take this."

Angela took the rifle without thanks, and Clint kicked Duke in the ribs and rode off.

"Why'd you give my mother that rifle?" Irene asked. "I thought you said those men wouldn't be back."

Clint hesitated a moment before saying, "There are all kinds of wild animals around here."

Walt Denver and Del Beman watched as Clint Adams and another rider rode up to the burning house and talked to the women there.

"What do you think?" Beman asked.

"Let's wait a minute," Denver said.

They watched until Clint Adams mounted up again and pulled one of the women up behind him on his horse.

"What now?" Beman asked.

"You ride back to the ranch and tell the boss that Adams was here."

"What are you gonna do?"

"I'm gonna follow them awhile and see what Adams has in mind."

"You know, we could ride down there now and—"

"Forget it," Denver said. "I'd do a lot of things for money, but killin' women ain't one of them. Go ahead. I'll be back to the ranch later."

"If you're not back by dark," Beman said, "we'll come lookin' for you."

"I'll be back," Denver said.

Chapter Twenty-Two

The ride back to the Press ranch was an uncomfortable one, to say the least: Clint was highly aware of Irene Dennison's firm young breasts digging into his back.

When they reached the ranch, Clint dismounted first, then reached up and helped Irene down. Before her feet had touched the ground, her arms were around his neck and she was kissing him.

"Irene . . ." he said, but she was insistent, and her lips were young and firm. And tasty. Before long her tongue was in his mouth.

They were in the barn, so no one was able to see them. Finally, Clint managed to disengage himself from her and stepped away.

He said the only thing he could think to say: "Irene, what would your mother say?"

"Mother isn't here, Clint," she said, reaching for him again.

"Irene," Clint said, grabbing her hands and holding them in his, "we don't have time for this now."

"When will we have time?" she asked.

"Never," he said. "You're very young, Irene."

"You're not so old," she said. "Besides, we all know you've slept with Katy and Sandy."

"How do you know that?" Clint asked. "Did they say anything?"

"Of course they didn't," Irene said, "but another woman can tell."

"You're hardly a woman yet, Irene."

"I'm not a virgin, Clint," she said. "And I'm eighteen."

"Let's talk about this another time, Irene," Clint said. "Your mother and the others are waiting."

Irene didn't seem convinced, but at that moment Pevy walked into the barn, and she backed away from Clint reluctantly.

"What's goin' on?"

Clint turned to the foreman. "The women have been burned out."

"By who?"

"They think it was Kennedy's men," Clint said. "One of them noticed the brand on the horses."

"Any of them hurt?"

"No," Clint said. "I want to send some horses out to them so they can come back here."

"I'll get that done."

"Also, I'd like to buy some lumber and build them something they can live in for a while."

"What do you intend to use for money?" Pevy asked.

"Doesn't Beverly have credit in town?"

"She has excellent credit," Pevy said. "And she'd like to keep it that way."

"Well," Clint said, "we don't have to build them a *big* house."

Pevy stared at him for a minute, then nodded. "All right, I'll have that taken care of, too."

"You take care of the lumber," Clint said, "and I'll take the horses out to them."

"What about me?" asked Irene.

"Is Mrs. Marshall in the house?" Clint asked Pevy.

"Yes," Pevy said. "She's ranting and raving about someone using her kitchen. Would you know anything about that?"

"Not a thing," Clint lied. "Would you have Mrs. Marshall show Irene to a room in the house?"

"Sure," Pevy said. "This way, ma'am."

"I know which way the house is," Irene said, and she stalked out of the barn.

Pevy turned to Clint. "Do you have any idea of the trouble you could be causing by bringing six women here?"

"They won't be here for long, Pevy," Clint said. "I doubt Kennedy will send his men in here after them."

"It's not Kennedy's men I'm worried about," Pevy said. "It's mine!"

"Can you have someone saddle five horses?"

"What are you gonna be doing?"

"We had company on the way back."

"Someone followed you?"

"Yeah," Clint said, "and I want to find out who it was."

"You need help?"

"No," Clint said. "There was only one. I think I can

handle it." He mounted up again. "Just have someone saddle those horses."

Clint wheeled Duke around and left the barn by the back door, hoping that the man on the hill above them wouldn't be able to see him until it was too late.

Walt Denver watched Clint Adams and the girl ride into the barn. A few minutes later, he saw Pevy walk into the barn and then the girl come out. After that he saw Pevy come out, but it had been more than ten minutes and Clint Adams still hadn't come out.

Unless he'd used a back door.

Denver rolled over onto his back and frantically looked around him. Off to the right, he spotted Clint Adams riding toward him. Cursing, he jumped up, mounted his horse, and sent him off at a gallop, hoping to outrun Adams.

Chapter Twenty-Three

It was clear after fifty yards that the man was not going to outrun Duke, so Clint just gave the big gelding his head and they ran the man down.

Neither one of them went for their guns, which suited Clint just fine. The man, once he realized he was caught, reined his horse in.

"You like burning women out of their homes?" Clint asked.

"I don't know what you're talking about."

"What's your name?" Clint asked.

"Denver," the man said, "Walt Denver."

"How long have you worked for Tom Kennedy?"

"About eight years."

"You came here with him, then?"

"That's right."

"You ever burned a bunch of women out of their homes for him before?"

"No, this was the first—hey, I-I don't know nothin' about that."

Clint reached out and stiff-armed the man so that he fell from his horse. He hit the ground hard, but to his credit he got to his feet immediately.

"You want to go for your gun?"

"Not against you, Adams," Denver said, spreading his hands wide, away from his guns. "That would be the same as suicide."

"Then you're lucky I need you alive," Clint said. "Give your boss a message for me."

"What message?"

"Tell him I wasn't working for the women before, but I am now," Clint said. "Tell him to keep his men away from them if he wants them to stay alive. Will you tell him that for me?"

"I'll tell him."

"Oh, yeah, and tell him the same goes for his hired gun."

"You won't be so high and mighty when Trey Hatcher gets here, Adams."

"You don't think so, eh?"

"Well," Denver said, "actually, I *do* think so. That is, I made a bet that you could take Hatcher."

"You bet on me?"

"That's right."

"Denver," Clint said, "that's probably the only thing you've done right since I met you. You and I might even become friends."

"I doubt it."

"Don't forget, Walt," Clint said, "give my message to Kennedy."

"I'll give it to him."

As Clint rode off, Denver rubbed his chest where the Gunsmith had stiff-armed him. It would almost be worth losing his bet to see Clint Adams get his.

Trey Hatcher drained his coffee cup, then put out the fire with the remains in the pot. He stood up and kicked dirt onto the dead fire to make sure it stayed dead, and then he stowed his gear away. After that, he saddled his horse and mounted up.

His original intention had been to camp longer, but he figured that by riding straight through he could get to Little Creek almost a full day early.

He couldn't wait to be standing opposite Clint Adams—and his reputation.

That would even be worth riding through the night and having beef jerky for dinner.

It might even mean riding his horse into the ground.

That was okay, too.

Once he killed the Gunsmith, he could help himself to the man's horse as well as his reputation.

Chapter Twenty-Four

When Clint arrived at the burnt-out house with the five horses, Katy and Sandy eagerly took the reins of two of them.

Clint walked a horse over to Alice Williams and handed her the reins.

"Where's Angela?" he asked.

"She's behind the house," Alice said. "She's not going to come, you know."

"You get going," Clint said. "I'll talk to her."

"You can talk all you want," Alice said, "but she's not coming."

"Maybe you should talk to her."

"Me?" the older woman asked. "I've already talked to her, Mr. Adams, over and over again. I haven't ever been able to change her mind about anything. That's one hard woman, Mr. Adams."

Sandy and Katy had already ridden off. Clint looked over at Bonnie Franks. "Can Bonnie ride?" he asked.

"Not very well," Alice said. "I'll ride along with

her, though. I think I can keep her from falling off."

"Just pick one of the other horses for her and leave," Clint said. "I'll see what I can do about Angela."

Alice Williams laughed without humor and said, "Good luck to you."

Clint watched as Alice helped Bonnie up onto one of the horses and the two women rode off. He took the reins of the remaining horse and walked around and behind what was left of the house. Though it was still standing, it was a burnt-out hulk that would keel over as soon as someone leaned on it or as soon as a good stiff wind came along.

Angela Dennison was down on her haunches, staring off into space.

"Mrs. Dennison?"

She turned her head and looked at him.

"Oh, it's all right for you to call me Angela, Mr. Adams," she said. "After all, you are helping us to survive here, aren't you?"

"And that sticks in your craw so badly?" Clint asked.

"You bet it does," she said, standing up. "I left New Jersey to get away from the men who were running my life."

"And why did the others leave?"

"Before I tell you that," she said, "let me tell you what we used to do back in New Jersey."

"I know what you used to do."

"You *think* you know."

"Yes," he said, "I think I know."

Actually, when he thought about it, it wasn't too hard to figure, especially considering the skill with which both Katy and Sandy had performed in bed.

"Well, go ahead," Angela said, "make your best guess."

Clint decided not to be delicate. "You were whores," he said. "At least some of you were."

"All of us were," Angela said. "Except for my daughter, Irene." To her credit, Angela managed to cover up the surprise she'd felt after he had guessed right.

"And you took her away from New Jersey to *keep* her from becoming one?" Clint asked.

"That was one of the reasons," Angela said. "In New Jersey most of the whorehouses are run by men, not madams, like out here."

"You got tired of having men tell you what to do?"

"What to do," she said, "where to do it, how to do it. I got tired of fat, sweaty businessmen putting their hands all over me, and . . . I got tired of it, that's all."

"And the others?"

"All right, so I bullied them into coming with me," Angela said. "Alice and I have been friends for a long time. Bonnie and Irene are friends."

"Katy and Sandy?"

"Sandy was tired of being a whore," Angela said. "She didn't hate it, like I did, but she wanted to get away from it."

"And Katy?"

"You know," Angela said, "I'm not sure about that at all. I guess you'll have to ask her."

"I guess I will."

"So," Angela said, "you had two of the girls. You think I'm going to be the third?"

"The thought never crossed my mind," Clint said.

"I'll leave this horse here for you. There's a blanket on the saddle."

"Do you think I'll use it?"

"The blanket or the horse?"

"The horse, damn it."

"I hope you will," Clint said. "When it gets cold enough, you'll use the blanket."

He dropped the horse's reins and started to walk away. He turned back and said, "I hope you won't let your pride keep you here."

"Maybe my pride is all I've got left," Angela said.

"I think you've got more than that."

"Like what?"

"You've got a daughter, you've got friends," Clint said, "and you've got people who are willing to help you—if you decide you want help. That's a hell of a lot more than most people have in a lifetime."

He turned and walked to Duke. When he mounted up, he waited a moment to see if she would appear from behind the house. When she did not, he rode off, back to the Press ranch.

Chapter Twenty-Five

In order to accommodate all the guests, Clint moved back into Beverly's room. The room he'd had was now being shared by Bonnie Franks and Irene Dennison. There were enough rooms so that Alice Williams, Katy Brennan, and Sandy Ward could each have their own.

Mrs. Marshall, still convinced that someone had "violated" her kitchen while she was away, prepared dinner for the five women and Clint. Clint also asked Pevy if he would join them.

"Don't think you can handle all those women?" Pevy asked.

"I know I can't."

"I'll be there."

After dinner Clint decided to ask them all a question he'd been wanting to ask.

"Ladies, if I can have your attention," he said as Mrs. Marshall was serving coffee.

The last to look at him was Alice Williams. She and Pevy were sitting next to each other, and they seemed to have struck up a friendship.

"Now that you're all here and Angela isn't," Clint said, "I'd like to ask you all something."

"Something you don't think we'd answer if Angela *was* here?" Sandy asked.

"That's right."

"You're assuming we're all afraid of Angela?" Sandy asked.

"Not afraid," Clint said, "but I'm sure she's the reason most of you left New Jersey and came out here."

"She's the reason we *all* came out here," Alice Williams said. "What do you want to ask?"

"I'd like to know just how many of you are really willing to fight for the land you're on." He looked at them all in turn, and then said, "Alice?"

"Are you asking me first because I'm the oldest?" she asked.

"Before anyone answers that question," Katy said, "I'd like to know if you mean, whether we would be willing to fight with or without you."

"Does it make a difference?"

The women exchanged glances, and then Katy said, "I think it makes a big difference."

"I'm only one man."

"But what a man!" Sandy said, and the other women all looked at her. "I mean," she added, "look at his reputation."

"What do you know about my reputation?" Clint asked.

"Oh, come now, Clint," she said. "Even back east we've read about you."

"I never read about him," Bonnie said. "Who is he?"

"He's a real legend of the West, Bonnie," Katy said. "They call him the Gunsmith."

"Why?" Bonnie asked.

"I've asked myself that question, too," Clint said.

He waited patiently while Katy and Sandy explained to Bonnie and to Irene, who had also never heard of him, who he was.

"Ladies," Alice said, "let's remember how many miles those stories had to travel before they got to us."

"What's that got to do with it?" Katy asked.

"Reputations are like snowballs," Alice said. "The farther they travel, the bigger they become."

"Thank you, Alice," Clint said. "I've never heard that put any better."

"Thank *you*."

"You mean he's not the Gunsmith?" Bonnie asked, looking confused.

"Yes, he is the Gunsmith," Alice said. "All I'm saying is—"

"I think the issue is getting confused," Clint said, cutting her off. "My original question stands: How many of you are willing to fight for this land against Kennedy and his men?"

There was a long period of silence then as each woman considered the question.

"Alice?" Clint said.

"I'm too old to be running away to fight another day," she said.

"You ain't that old," Pevy said.

She patted his hand. "You're sweet."

Alice was about five years older than Pevy, but that didn't seem to affect the man's opinion.

"Sandy?"

Sandy shrugged. "Who's to say we won't run into the same problem someplace else? We might as well face it here."

"Irene?"

"I'll go along with my mother," she said. "If she stays, I'll stay."

"Then how come you're not out there with her tonight?" Katy asked sweetly.

"Katy—"

"Let's leave the arguing until later," Clint said. "What about you, Bonnie?"

Bonnie stared around the table wide-eyed and said, "I'll go along with the majority."

"And you, Katy?"

"Well, to tell you the truth," she said, "I wouldn't mind moving on, if I had someone to move on with."

"Do you?" Irene asked.

"Not at the moment, dear," Katy said, "so I guess I'll stay."

"Regardless of how large or small your reputation is, Clint," Alice said, "will we be standing with just you against Kennedy and his men?"

"I reckon that would be up to me and my men," Pevy said.

"How so?" Alice asked.

"Well," Pevy said, "Clint stands alone only if we don't back him."

"And why would you?" Alice asked. "This is partly his fight because someone tried to kill him, but why would it be your fight?"

"It would be my fight," Pevy said, "if I make it my fight."

"And why would you do that?" Alice was persistent.

" 'Cause Clint is a friend of mine," Pevy said, which Clint knew was a lie, "and because somebody tried to kill him here, at my ranch."

"*Your* ranch?" Katy asked.

"Pevy is speaking as foreman," Clint said, "and in Beverly's absence, the ranch is as good as his."

"Then you and your men will help?" Sandy asked.

"I will," Pevy said. "I can't order my men to, but I think they'll go along with me."

"This is starting to sound exciting," Sandy said. "Tell me, is this what's known as a range war?"

"Not quite," Pevy said.

Chapter Twenty-Six

After the women had all retired for the night, Clint and Pevy went into Beverly's office for a glass of brandy.

"What do you think?" Clint asked.

"I think that Alice is some kind of lady," Pevy said. "Mature, and smart—"

"I meant about all of them," Clint said. "You willing to stand with me against Kennedy for them?"

"A couple of them didn't sound real enthusiastic about fighting for their home," Pevy admitted, "but from what I heard, this Angela seems real intent on it."

"Alice and Sandy seem to be also. Irene will stand with her mother. Bonnie just seems a little too meek to make up her own mind, so she'll go along with the rest."

"And Katy?"

"Katy is . . . well, she's Katy. She's got her own reasons for doing what she does."

"You think Mrs. Dennison will be all right out there by herself?" Pevy asked.

"I was thinking the same thing," Clint said. "Maybe I'll take a ride out there and look in on her."

"I could send a man—"

"No, no," Clint said. "I'll do it myself."

"Ain't you tired?"

Clint smiled. "Could you sleep with five attractive women on the same floor with *you*?"

"Well, I'd only be tempted by Alice," Pevy said, "but I see your point."

"Maybe I should stay here and watch you," Clint said.

"I don't need watching," Pevy said. "Besides, if I *wanted* to go up there to her room, you couldn't stop me."

"I wouldn't want to," Clint said. "It's the second door on the left, and she's alone."

"Thanks for the information," Pevy said, setting his glass down. "I better get out of here before I use it. Good night."

"Good night, Pevy."

"You want me to have someone saddle your horse?"

"No, just let the men on watch know that I might be riding out, so they don't shoot me."

"I'll tell 'em. Good night."

As Pevy left, Clint poured himself another glass of brandy and thought about the women up on the second floor. If he went to his room he wondered if there'd be a knock on his door at some point. Sandy, Katy, maybe even Irene might decide to sneak down to his room. And what would happen if he let one of them in? Would one of the others come along later? It just wasn't safe to go up there—not just yet. Riding out to look in on Angela seemed the reasonable thing to do.

"Would you mind if I had a glass of that?"

He turned and saw Alice Williams standing in the doorway.

"Of course not," he said. "Come on in."

She was wearing a robe belted tightly around her waist. It accentuated the full thrust of her breasts, and he was reminded once again that even at fifty— or more—she was a handsome figure of a woman.

She came into the room and accepted a glass of brandy from him.

"Can I ask you something?" she asked.

"Go ahead."

"What's all this going to come to?"

He knew what she meant. With Kennedy and all his men against Pevy and all his men, a lot of people could end up dead.

"To tell you the truth, Alice," Clint said, "I believe it will come down to Trey Hatcher and me."

"This Trey Hatcher," she said. "Does he have a reputation too?"

"Yes."

"Like yours?"

"Not yet, but he's trying."

"And he thinks that killing you will give him that bigger reputation?"

"That's usually the way it works."

"Did it work that way with you?"

"Uh, no," Clint said. "I'm afraid I got my reputation the hard way. I didn't kill any one man with a big rep to get it. That's a shortcut the young are always trying to use."

"You were young once," she said.

"I don't think I was ever *that* young."

"So we just wait around for this gunman to get here, and then either he kills you or you kill him."

"That's the way I feel it will go."

"Can't the law do anything?"

"I'm pretty certain the sheriff is working for Tom Kennedy."

She stared into her brandy glass for a few moments, then said, "Maybe we should move on then."

"Why?"

"I don't think that land is worth your life."

"There's more to it than that, Alice."

"Like what?"

"You have to remember that someone tried to kill me," he reminded her.

"But you killed him first."

"True, but he was working for someone."

"Kennedy?"

"He was on Kennedy's payroll at the time, but I think his friend, Teddy Rigg, sent him after me."

"And you want Teddy Rigg?"

"Yes."

"Why?"

"Because, like it or not, I have a reputation," he explained. "If Teddy Rigg starts telling people that he had someone try to kill me and got away with it, I'll have even more youngsters coming after me, thinking I've gone soft."

Alice looked stunned for a moment.

"I had no idea you had to live like that," she said. "Don't you get tired?"

"Extremely."

She moved closer to him, and her scent found its way into his nostrils. It wasn't perfume; it was just her, and it was pleasant.

"Have you ever thought of chucking it all and going away?"

"I've done that."

"And what happened?"

He smiled and shrugged fatalistically. "It always catches up to me."

"So with all of that, you still find time to fight other people's battles?"

"Only when they can't fight them alone."

She put her glass down on the desk and moved even closer to him.

"You're a special man, Clint Adams." She kissed him.

He kissed her back for a few seconds, then pulled his head away. She smiled at him and backed away. He had the feeling that she was silently laughing at him.

"Don't you worry, Clint Adams," she said, walking toward the door. "I'm just an old woman who wanted to see what I was missing. I'm not going to try to jump into your bed."

At the door she stopped, looked back at him, and said, "It's pretty crowded as it is, isn't it?"

As she left, he looked up at the ceiling and wondered how much she knew. Then he wondered what she knew that he didn't.

Was there already someone waiting for him up in his bed?

He decided a ride out to check on Angela might be just the thing.

Chapter Twenty-Seven

Angela Dennison wished she had gone back to the Press ranch with the others. That would have been admitting weakness, though, and after months of trying to be strong, that was something she didn't want to admit to.

So what was she doing now, trying to find the Press ranch in the dark?

Sitting in front of that burnt-out hulk had finally gotten to her, along with the chill in the air that seemed to go right through the damned blanket Clint Adams had left her.

Clint Adams.

She was going to have to face the look on his face, as well as the faces of the others, when she finally did find the house. What would Irene think of her mother when she came riding in with her tail between her legs?

Damn, but she was tired of being strong. Just once she wanted to melt into someone's arms and just stay there for a while—maybe someone like Clint Adams. He had proven several times that he was nothing like the men she had left behind in New Jersey. So why did she insist on treating him so badly?

She stopped at the top of a rise and glanced around her. The moon was just a sliver and wasn't affording her that much light. The horse began to pull at the reins, and she decided to give him his head. Maybe he knew the way back to the ranch.

As it turned out, the horse was just thirsty and took her to a water hole.

"All right, damn it," she said. She dismounted and let him go. "Drink your fill."

The horse walked to the edge of the water and lowered his head to drink. She decided that she might as well get a drink too.

She moved farther along, away from the horse, and got to her knees. As she put her hands in the water, someone touched her. She jerked her hands back, then decided it must have been her imagination. Gingerly, she put her hands back into the water, and again it felt as if someone had touched her hands.

She moved her hand around in the water and finally encountered what felt like another hand—below the surface of the water.

Another hand.

Five fingers and all, right there under the water.

God!

Clint heard the scream, and it came from nearby.

"Come on, boy," he said, urging Duke on.

He remembered that there was a water hole nearby, and he directed Duke toward it. He saw the horse first, then the figure kneeling at the water's edge. He dismounted and ran forward. He didn't recognize her at first.

"Angela?"

She didn't answer.

"Angela," he said, coming up behind her and touching her shoulders, "what is it?"

She turned her head and looked at him, then pointed into the water. He saw something there just beneath the surface.

"Come on, get up," he said. He got her to her feet and walked her away from the water. "Stay here."

She nodded, and he went back to the water's edge. He reached into the water and felt a hand there. He grabbed it and pulled. It felt as if the body were stuck on something, and he pulled harder. Finally, the hand broke the surface of the water, followed by a head. Before long he had the body completely out of the water. It hadn't been stuck on anything. Its clothes had been stuffed with rocks to weight it down. The arm and hand must have come loose and floated to the top.

"What is it?" she asked from behind him. She was craning her neck, at the same time wanting to see and *not* wanting to see what it was.

"Not *what*," he said over his shoulder, "*who*. It's a man's body."

"A man?" she asked. She sounded closer to him now as she inched forward to have a look. "Well then, do you know who it is?"

He rolled the body over and brushed the hair away from its face.

"Jesus . . ."

Bloated as it was, he still managed to recognize the face.

"Do you know who it is?" she asked again.

"Yeah," Clint said, releasing the body so that it rolled back over onto its stomach. "I know who it is, all right."

Not only was it bloated from being in the water, but there was a bullet hole in the head. Still, he was able to identify the body.

He stared down at the body of Teddy Rigg.

"Well, Teddy," he said softly, "I guess when Tom Kennedy fires somebody, he really fires them."

Chapter Twenty-Eight

Clint gave Angela Dennison two choices.

"We could camp here for the night and make a fire, or we could go back to the ranch."

"I'm not staying here with that," she said, indicating the body.

"That means we go back," Clint said. "That is, if it was the ranch you were heading for."

She lifted her chin defiantly. "It was."

"Then let's go."

"What about . . . that?"

"We'll send someone out in the morning to pick up the body."

"And then what?"

"And then we'll take it into town. Not that it will do much good to tell the sheriff what I think happened."

"Why not?"

"I'm pretty sure he's working for Kennedy."

"Oh, that's great."

They mounted up and headed back to the Press ranch.

"Where were you headed?" she asked him.

"Me?" He considered lying, then decided to tell her the truth. "I was just riding out to see how you were doing."

"Is that so?"

"Yes."

"Why?"

"I figured you might need some company, if not another blanket."

There was a moment of silence, and then she said, "I *was* getting kind of lonely."

"We could go back there, if you want, and I could keep you company."

"No, that's all right," she said. "I hope you, uh, have room for me at the house."

"You'll have to share a room, and a bed, with either Katy, Sandy, or Alice."

"Not with you?" Her tone indicated that she must have been feeling better, because the bitterness was back.

"That's not one of the choices," he said.

They rode along in silence a ways, and then she asked, "Was that one of the men who was harassing Katy and Bonnie in town?"

"Yes."

"Is he the one who sent the man to kill you?"

"Yes."

"Well then, if he's dead, I guess you'll be moving on. I mean, it *was* him you were looking for, wasn't it?"

"It was," he said, "but I went through this whole

thing once already tonight. One of the other girls can fill you in on the details."

"All right," she said. "I won't press you."

"Thanks."

"If the sheriff is working for Kennedy, what kind of chance do we have in this county—legally, I mean."

"To keep your property? A pretty good one, I think," Clint said. "The sheriff can enforce the law, and he can enforce it selectively, but he can't change it."

"So, legally, we have no problem," she said, "but we still have to withstand Kennedy and his men."

This time, even though he'd been through it already, he explained about Trey Hatcher.

"Just like in the stories."

"What stories?"

"The stories we read about the West, back in New Jersey. The two men facing each other on the dusty street, both drawing their weapons, one lying in the dirt while the other one walks away. Like that?"

"It's not usually like that," he said. "I mean—well, the streets *are* usually dusty."

She gave him a sideways look to see if he were teasing her, and when he started to laugh she had to smile.

"Seriously, what happens if you kill Hatcher?"

"That will have been Kennedy's best shot to get me out of the way," he said. "I think he'll back off if that happens."

"And if Hatcher kills you?"

"Then I think you and your friends would be well advised to move on."

"And leave our land?"

"Sell it to Kennedy," he said. "You won't get as good a price as he originally offered you, but you'll get something."

"So why should we wait until you're dead to do that?" she asked.

"Because while I'm alive there's a chance you won't have to sell."

She thought that over for a few minutes, then asked, "That doesn't sound fair to you?"

"Really?"

"I'm serious," she said. "If there's a chance you could be killed, why don't we just sell it to him now and move on?"

"You'd do that for me?"

"I'd—well, not for you—I mean, at this point I'd do it for the sake of anyone's life."

"What about yours?"

"Do you think Kennedy would really kill us?"

"No, I don't," Clint said. "If he was going to do that, he had the perfect opportunity today. Also, it takes a special breed of man to kill a woman—or a bunch of women—for money."

"Are you saying the breed doesn't exist?"

"No, I'm just saying that they may take a while to find, but a man with money can find them. Sometimes you just have to offer a man enough money, and he'll do anything."

She hesitated a moment, then said, "The same goes for some women."

He wondered then if she were thinking about some of the things she may have done for money in the past.

"I suppose I should thank you," she said.

"Only if you want to."

There was a long moment of silence, and then she said, "Thank you."

He laughed.

"What's so funny?"

"That sounded like you had to drag it out."

She stared at him for a moment, and then she had to laugh.

"Actually, I did, but now that it's been said, it doesn't seem so bad."

"Good," he said, "I'm glad. Maybe we can be friends after this and start working together."

It was her turn to laugh now.

"What do *you* find so funny?"

"It's just that I've never met a man who only wanted to be my friend," she said. "They usually just want to go to bed with me and then forget me."

"I'd rather *not* go to bed with you than forget you," Clint said.

"Why?"

"If friends are worth making," he said, "they're worth remembering."

"You know," she said, "you're really making me think that I've been wrong about you."

"Good," he said. "Then we've accomplished something very important tonight."

"I suppose we have."

Clint called out to the man on watch and they were allowed to approach the house.

"I see you're being careful."

"Very," Clint said. "We have three men on watch at all times."

"Then you are worried about Kennedy and his men?"

"Not Kennedy," Clint said. "But some of his men might act rashly. I'm just guarding against stupidity."

They rode to the barn, where Clint unsaddled both horses and saw to them while Angela waited.

"Come on," he said. "Let's see if we can find you something to eat."

"Oh, I'm not that hungry," she said. "Maybe I'll just turn in."

"Who do you want to share with?"

She thought a moment. "Oh, Alice, I guess."

"Uh, there's a possibility that Alice might have company," he said.

"Really?"

"Don't get angry."

"Oh, I'm not angry," Angela said. "Not any more. That part of the agreement is good and dead—thanks, in part, to you."

"Now, Angela—"

"Never mind, Clint," she said. "You don't have to explain. You're an attractive man, and Katy and Sandy—well, it's a wonder they lasted as long as they did."

"What about you?"

"You mean, do I think you're attractive?" she asked. "Are you going to ruin our budding friendship by inviting me to your bed?"

"No," Clint said, "that's not what I meant at all."

She smiled. "I'm glad," she said, and went upstairs.

Chapter Twenty-Nine

Tom Kennedy had thrown Walt Denver and Del Beman out of his office. Denver had been dumb enough to follow Clint Adams and then be caught doing it.

"Just stay away from him and those women until Hatcher gets here," he told them.

"Look, Boss, I'm sorry—" Denver started.

"Just get out, Walt," Kennedy said.

"Boss—" Beman began, but he had no chance to speak further.

"You too, Del," Kennedy said. "Get out! And stay away from them!"

After both men had left, Kennedy poured himself a brandy before retiring. He was just going to have to steer clear of Adams until Trey Hatcher got to town. Since it was after midnight, that would probably be tomorrow.

One more day, and Clint Adams would be a memory—providing Trey Hatcher was as good as he was supposed to be. Kennedy had used Hatcher before, but he'd never seen Hatcher go up against anyone like the Gunsmith.

It was going to be real interesting.

Chapter Thirty

By noon they had the lumber out by the burnt-out house and had pulled the empty hulk down. Clint had ridden into town with the men for the lumber, and they had taken the body of Teddy Rigg in with them. The sheriff had reacted much the same way in which he'd reacted to Frank Lobo's body: He wasn't interested.

He did say to Clint, "You have a habit of finding bodies."

"Sheriff," Clint had said, "you ought to be more interested in whoever's *making* them."

"What are we putting up here?" one of the men asked Pevy.

Pevy looked at Clint, who said, "Just something to give them shelter from the weather."

"How many rooms?" the man asked.

Clint turned to Angela and repeated the question.

"Nothing fancy," she said. "Just a dozen rooms or so."

143

"What!" the man asked.

"Two," Clint said. "Make two rooms."

"All right."

The man's name was Kyle Bodeen, and he apparently had some background in construction. Clint wondered if they were going to end up with something better than even he had envisioned.

Pevy had cut loose six men to work on the house, and the six women were doing what they could to help.

"I've got to get back to the ranch," Pevy said to Clint. "What are you gonna do?"

"I don't know," Clint said. "They seem to have everything under control here."

"Kyle knows what he's doing," Pevy said. "You might as well come back with me."

"And do what?" Clint asked as they mounted up. "Maybe I'll go into town."

"To wait for Hatcher?"

Clint shrugged. "The faster we get it over with, the faster I can move on."

"Tired of it here, huh?" Pevy asked.

"It just hasn't been as restful as I thought it would be."

"It'll be pretty damned restful if Trey Hatcher kills you."

"Well, I figure maybe I can talk to him."

"Talk to a killer?"

"All we know about him is his reputation," Clint said, "and we know what that's worth."

"Somehow the image of Trey Hatcher and the Gunsmith talkin' just doesn't sit well with me."

"We'll try it that way first, Pevy, and see what happens."

"Suit yourself."

"If I was going to do that," Clint said, "I would have left right after Beverly did."

By the time Trey Hatcher rode into town, most of the townspeople knew he was coming. Not many of them knew that the stranger riding into town actually *was* Hatcher, but he *was* a stranger, so they stared.

Hatcher rode directly to the livery, ignoring the stares of the people on the street. He left his horse there and then took his gear and walked to the hotel.

When he walked into the hotel, the clerk stared openly at the dusty, bedraggled man. Hatcher slammed his saddlebags down on the desk, raising a cloud of dust.

"A room," he said.

"S-sure, sure," the clerk said. "Take any one you like."

"Give me the register."

The clerk turned the register around, never taking his eyes off Hatcher's face. Hatcher signed his name and turned the book back around.

"Key."

The clerk reached behind him without looking and took a key off the board.

"I'm gonna sleep for six hours," Hatcher said. "I don't want to be disturbed. Understand?"

"Yes, sir."

Hatcher picked up his saddlebags and went up to

his room. After he was gone, some people crowded into the lobby.

"Was that him?" someone asked the clerk.

"That was him," the clerk said, looking at the register. "There it is, bold as day. Trey Hatcher."

"What was he like?" someone else asked.

"A killer," the clerk said. "If I ever saw the face of a killer, he had it."

"When was the last time *you* saw the face of a killer, Barney?" someone said.

"Just a couple of seconds ago," the clerk answered.

When Clint Adams rode into town a few hours later, he could still feel the excitement in the air. He'd seen towns react this way before when Bill Hickok would ride in. It usually lasted for hours, sometimes days.

He knew instinctively that Trey Hatcher had arrived in town.

He rode to the sheriff's office and dismounted there.

"Sheriff," he called as he entered.

"Adams!" Sheriff Ransom said. "What are you doing in town?"

"He's here, isn't he?"

Ransom nodded. "He's over at the hotel, sleeping."

"The hotel, huh?"

"You gonna sneak over there and shoot him in bed?" Ransom asked.

"Why would I want to do that?" Clint asked.

"He's here to kill you, you know."

"I just want to talk to him."

"Sure."

"I don't want to kill him if I don't have to, Sheriff," Clint said.

"You mean you don't want him to kill you."

"That too," Clint said. "If it comes to that, you intend to do anything to stop it?"

"What can I do?"

"You'll do exactly what Tom Kennedy tells you to do, won't you?"

"Listen, Adams—"

"Never mind, Sheriff," Clint said. "Never mind. You've probably already sent word to Tom Kennedy that his man is here."

As a matter of fact, the sheriff had sent Sammy Judd out to the Kennedy ranch as soon as he'd heard that Hatcher had arrived.

"Sure you did," Clint said. "I'm going to tell you this just once. If you're not going to do anything to stop it, don't get in my way. You understand?"

"I-I understand," Ransom said.

"In fact," Clint said, "it would be safer for you if you'd just stay inside."

"Stay inside," Ransom said. "I understand."

"I'm going over to talk to Hatcher now. If you see Kennedy, tell him the same thing I told you: Stay out of my way."

"I'll tell him."

Clint gave the "lawman" a disgusted look, then turned and left the office.

He walked Duke over to the hotel and left him outside. Inside there were a few people around the front desk, and the clerk seemed to be the center of attention.

"He stood right where you're standing, and he had

death in his eyes. I never been so close to a killer before."

Clint moved in among the crowd and faced the clerk.

"What room is Trey Hatcher in?"

The clerk stopped his story and looked at Clint.

"Mr. Hatcher can't be disturbed right now. He's ridden a long way, and he needs his rest."

"Just tell me what room he's in."

"I told you, sir," the clerk said, "he doesn't want to see anyone."

Clint reached across and grabbed the front of the clerk's shirt, pulling him halfway across the desk.

"He'll see me," Clint said. "He *came* here to see me."

The clerk's eyes widened. He had seen this man around town, but until now he hadn't known who he was.

"You're the Gunsmith?"

"That's right."

The people crowding around the desk moved back several steps, staring at Clint.

"What room is he in?" Clint asked again.

The clerk had to look behind him to check the key board.

"He's in room five," he said. "You gonna kill him in his sleep?"

Clint pushed the clerk back violently and whirled on the other people.

"Get out of here!" he shouted. "Go on about your business!"

The men backed away from him and then hurried out the door. Behind the desk the clerk stared at Clint

Adams, waiting for the Gunsmith to kill him.

"I'm going upstairs," Clint said. "When I come down, I don't want to see you."

The clerk nodded, and as Clint Adams mounted the steps, he ran out from behind the desk.

He'd survived two killers in one day. He was going to be a real celebrity in this town after today.

Chapter Thirty-One

Clint moved cautiously down the hall toward room five. His gun was in his holster, but he wasn't sure he was going to leave it there. It might be necessary to cover Trey Hatcher in order to get him to talk.

Clint realized that he had a preconceived notion of the kind of man Hatcher would be from his reputation, and he scolded himself for that. He'd been fighting that same prejudice himself for years.

When he reached room five, he decided to play it very simply.

He knocked.

"Go away."

He knocked again.

"I said I didn't want to be disturbed!"

"Hatcher," Clint called, "it's Clint Adams. Open up."

There was a moment of complete silence, and then he heard footsteps approaching the door.

"Adams," Hatcher said, "come in. Come on in."

Clint entered the room and looked Trey Hatcher over. He was tall and slender, still wearing the trail clothes he'd ridden in with. On top of being dusty, they were wrinkled because he'd been lying down in them.

"I'd offer to shake your hand," Hatcher said, "but I ain't cleaned up yet. To tell you the truth, I was in so much of a hurry to get here that I rode through the night. I really needed a few hours' sleep."

"Sorry to interrupt you," Clint said, "but I thought we needed to talk."

He saw Hatcher's gun hanging on the bedpost, and the younger man didn't seem to be giving it much attention.

"Well, good," Hatcher said, "we've got a lot to talk about. But how about you give me time to clean up? Then we can get something to eat together."

"Something to eat?"

"Sure," Hatcher said. "Hey, we both know why I'm here, Clint—can I call you Clint? There's no reason why we can't be civilized about it, right?"

"Right."

"Sure," Hatcher said. "Let me take a bath and I'll meet you in the lobby in an hour. We can get an early supper."

"All right," Clint said. "An hour."

Hatcher opened the door and said, "I'm glad you came up here, Clint. I've looked up to you for a lot of years."

"Is that so?"

"Believe me," Hatcher said, "it's true. But we can talk more in an hour."

"In an hour."

Clint walked back down the hall, pleasantly surprised by Trey Hatcher's attitude. Maybe it wouldn't
be so hard to talk some sense into him after all.

Hatcher prepared for his bath, humming a tune.
Having the Gunsmith come to him was more than
he could have asked for. What he had told Clint was
the truth: He *had* admired him for years. To have a
chance to actually *talk* to the man before killing him
was icing on the cake.

First there was the money, and then the opportunity
to add to his own reputation.

Now he was actually going to be able to talk to the
Gunsmith, observe him, and learn from him.

What more could a budding legend ask for?

When Clint got downstairs, the lobby was deserted.
The clerk had cleared out, probably frightened by his
threat. He wasn't very proud of himself for that.

To get to his bath Hatcher was probably going to
have to come through the lobby, and Clint didn't want
to be sitting there when he did. He decided to go to
the saloon and nurse a beer until it was time to meet
the man.

Now that he'd had a short conversation with Hatcher, he felt better about the whole situation.

Chapter Thirty-Two

"Not a chance," Trey Hatcher said.

"What?"

"I said there's not a chance of me leaving here without killing you."

"Or being killed."

"That too," Hatcher said. "Believe me, Clint, only one of us is going to leave this town."

It didn't make sense to Clint. He had met Hatcher in the hotel lobby and they had walked to the small cafe together to have a meal. Their conversation over supper could even have been called pleasant. The man was very interested in Clint's life—his "career," as he called it. Clint, unwilling to talk about himself, nevertheless found himself telling the engaging young man more than he had intended.

Then, when the subject came to the situation at hand, Trey Hatcher had said, "Not a chance."

"I don't understand this," Clint said. "You're an intelligent man."

"I know I am," Hatcher said. "I ain't educated, but I'm intelligent."

"You know right from wrong."

"Of course."

"Can't you see this is wrong?"

"For you, maybe," Trey Hatcher said. "For me, nothing could be righter."

Clint stared across the table at the man, who was very calm and collected while they talked about the possibility of one killing the other.

"Look, Trey," Clint said, "tell Kennedy to do his own killing."

"That doesn't matter," Hatcher said. "I'm not doing this for the money. Well, not *only* for the money. Do you know what killing the Gunsmith will do for me?"

"Yes, I do," Clint said. "It will make you a marked man, a target for every would-be gunman in the country. Is that what you want?"

Hatcher thought it over, then smiled and said, "Yeah, that's exactly what I want."

"Trey . . ." Clint said, shaking his head.

"Look," Hatcher said, "we'll do it tomorrow, all right? Leave this to me—I'll buy supper. It was a real pleasure talking to you. It meant a lot to me."

Trey Hatcher stood up.

"There is one thing, though."

"What's that?"

"I don't want to see you again until tomorrow. I'd hate to have to kill you when you're still digesting a meal that I bought you. Besides, I've got to see Kennedy this evening. Can you tell me how to get out to his ranch?"

"I don't think you'll have to," Clint said. "He'll be in here soon enough."

"Oh, well, fine," Hatcher said. "I'll wait for him. Thanks, Clint."

"Trey," Clint said, "is there anything I can say or do—"

"Nothing," Hatcher said. "Look, I know you ain't scared, so why don't you want to do this?"

"I don't want to kill you."

Hatcher smiled. "That's more like it," he said. "That's the kind of talk I'd expect from the Gunsmith."

Hatcher pushed his chair in and dropped some money on the table.

"Remember," he said, shaking his index finger at Clint, "I don't want to see you before tomorrow."

"Any particular time tomorrow?" Clint asked wearily.

"You mean like sunup?" Hatcher asked, laughing. "Isn't that only in the penny dreadfuls? No, Clint, just the first time we see each other, be ready."

"I'll be ready."

"I know you will. Until then."

Clint watched Hatcher walk from the cafe, and then the waiter came over to the table.

"Anything else, sir?"

"Yeah," Clint said, "another pot of coffee. I've got time to kill."

He winced as he realized his poor choice of words.

Tom Kennedy rode into town with Walt Denver and Del Beman just in time to see Clint Adams and Trey Hatcher walking into the cafe together.

"What the hell!" Walt Denver said.

"Is that Hatcher?" Beman asked.

"He matches the description," Denver said.

"But what the hell are they doin' together?" Beman asked. "Mr. Kennedy, do you see—"

"I see it, dammit!" Kennedy said. "There's got to be a reason."

"Like what?"

"We'll go to the hotel," Kennedy said, "wait for Hatcher, and then ask him."

When Trey Hatcher left the cafe he was a contented man: good company, a good meal in his belly, and a day to look forward to.

As he entered the hotel, he saw the three men waiting in the lobby. The clerk was still gone from behind the desk. He had to assume that the men were waiting for him.

One of the men was sitting while the other two flanked him. That told him that the seated man was Tom Kennedy, his employer.

As he entered, the seated man stood up and demanded loudly, "Just what the hell were you doing in the cafe with Clint Adams?"

"Are you Tom Kennedy?" Hatcher asked.

"I am."

"We'll talk upstairs, Mr. Kennedy," Hatcher said.

He started for the stairs. When he reached them, he turned and saw Kennedy following him, his two watchdogs following behind.

"They can stay down here."

Kennedy stopped and looked back at his men.

"Believe me, Kennedy," Hatcher said, "if I wanted

to kill you in my room, they couldn't stop me anyway. Also, they'd probably also end up dead." He mounted one step, then turned and said, "We're just going to talk."

Kennedy hesitated as Hatcher continued up the stairs, then turned to his men and said, "Wait here."

Chapter Thirty-Three

Hatcher closed the door to his room, then grabbed Kennedy by the front of his jacket and slammed him against the door hard enough to knock his hat off— but not much harder.

"H-hey—" Kennedy said.

"If we're going to get along," Hatcher said, "you're going to have to learn that you *never* talk to me like that in front of anyone—*ever!*"

The mad gleam that had crept into Trey Hatcher's eyes struck Kennedy speechless for a long moment, so that he found himself nodding jerkily.

"Y-yes, a-all right," Kennedy said. "I understand."

"Good," Hatcher said. He released his hold on Kennedy and backed away from him. "Now, you asked me a question in the lobby?"

"Yes," Kennedy said, straightening his jacket and picking up his hat. "I wondered what you were doing in the cafe with Clint Adams, the man I hired you to kill."

"I was having supper," Hatcher said. "And I was having the best conversation of my life. You see, the Gunsmith has been an idol of mine for years."

Kennedy frowned. "Does that mean—"

"No," Hatcher said, "that doesn't mean that I'm not going to kill him. I am."

"When?"

"Tomorrow."

"When tomorrow?"

"At the first moment we see each other."

"What if you don't see each other?"

Hatcher laughed. "We will."

"What did you talk about?"

"Not much," Hatcher said. "We talked about his past, about mine."

"Not the present?"

"What about the present?"

"I don't know."

"Are you worried that he told me what you're up to here?"

"Well . . ."

"I don't *care* what you're up to here, Kennedy," Hatcher said. "I don't even care if you're trying to push your own mother off her land. I'm here to kill the Gunsmith, period. After I do, you'll be happy, and so will I."

"And you'll be richer."

"For the experience, Kennedy," Hatcher said. "Your money is just what I need to keep on eating. Next question?"

"I don't have any more questions," Kennedy said. "You do your job, and I'll be around to pay you."

"You didn't come here without the money, did you, Kennedy?"

They exchanged stares for a few moments, and then Kennedy took an envelope out of his jacket pocket and handed it to Hatcher.

"I'll see you tomorrow, Kennedy," Hatcher said. "After the job is done."

"I'll be staying in town tonight," Kennedy said. He opened the door and said, "I wouldn't want to miss anything."

"I don't need an audience to do my job, Kennedy, but you stay around if you want. Just don't get in my way."

"Uh, you don't want a couple of my boys as, say, backup?"

Hatcher pinned Kennedy with a hard stare.

"Kennedy, if any of your boys so much as step onto the street tomorrow, I'll kill them first. Is that understood?"

"Understood," Kennedy said.

"Now get out."

Kennedy got out.

Down in the lobby, Kennedy called his men over.

"I'm staying overnight," he said to Beman. "Get me a room."

"Yes, sir."

"What did Hatcher say?" Denver asked.

"He admires the Gunsmith and looks up to him," Kennedy said. "He wanted a chance to talk to him before he killed him."

"But he's gonna do it?"

"Oh, he's gonna do it, all right," Kennedy said. "But I've got a job for you and Beman, if you want it."

"What job?" Beman asked, handing Kennedy a room key.

"After Hatcher kills Adams," Kennedy said, "I want the two of you to kill him."

"What?"

"I'll pay you five thousand dollars each."

"What about the law?"

"Don't worry about the law," Kennedy said. "I'll take care of the law; you just take care of Hatcher."

"But why?" Beman asked.

"Never mind, Boss," Denver said, nudging Beman. "We don't have to know why."

"Good," Kennedy said. "Bring my bag up to my room."

"Sure, Boss," Denver said.

After Kennedy had gone upstairs, Beman looked at Denver and said, "Why don't we have to know?"

"Five thousand dollars is reason enough for me," Denver said. "It should be reason enough for both of us, don't you think?"

"Sure, Walt," Beman said. "Sure."

"Let's get the boss's bag."

Chapter Thirty-Four

The situation was an odd one.

There was only one hotel in Little Creek, and once Clint had decided that he was going to spend the night in town, he, Trey Hatcher, and Tom Kennedy all ended up staying in the same place.

By the time Clint had made his decision, there was a new clerk on duty. He signed the register, accepted his key, and went up to his room.

He had stripped to the waist and was pulling off his boots when there was a knock on the door. He didn't bother guessing who it was; he just opened the door with an open mind.

It was Angela Dennison. Even if he *had* guessed, she would not have been among his top five.

"Can I come in?"

"Sure," Clint said. "I'm sorry. I'm just surprised to see you. Is everything all right?"

She entered the room. "Everything is fine."

"How's the house coming?"

"It's more than we could have hoped for," she said. "It'll be done late tomorrow."

"Where are the others?"

"Back at Beverly's ranch."

"So what are you doing here?"

"The truth?"

"Yes, the truth."

She surprised him even further by moving forward, lacing her fingers behind his neck, and kissing him, soundly and long.

"The truth is, if you're going to get killed tomorrow, I don't want to have to wonder what I missed."

"Well—" he began, but she cut him off with another kiss.

He turned her around without breaking the kiss and pulled her shirt out of her pants. When he had her shirt off and her breasts bare, he palmed them, popping the nipples between his fingers.

They helped each other disrobe entirely and then fell onto the bed, locked together. She ended up on top, and he traced the curve of her spine right into the crack between her ass cheeks, and he went further, until he got his finger wet. She gasped, then moved over him and came down on him, engulfing him.

She arched her back, jutting her breasts forward, and he reached up and clutched at them. They were firm and smooth, and the nipples were remarkably large and brown. She reached behind her and braced each of her hands on one of his knees and began to ride him that way. Her movements became faster and faster, and just as he exploded uncontrollably, she shuddered and cried out, and then she lay herself flat on him, her breasts mashed against his chest.

"Oh, my!" she said.

"What?"

"I would have been missing quite a lot, wouldn't I?" she whispered.

He laughed, and gathered her into his arms. "So would I."

Some time later she asked, "Have you talked to him?"

"Who?"

"Trey Hatcher."

"Oh, yeah, we talked."

"What did he say?"

"He said that only one of us was leaving this town alive."

"And what did you say?"

"I don't know," he said. "I might have said that it would be me and not him."

"Butting heads."

"What?"

"Like two rams butting heads."

"Or two bulls."

"Right," she said. "Whatever. Isn't there any way to stop it?"

"No."

"What about if we sold the land to Kennedy? Or gave it to him? Would he call Hatcher off?"

"He might, but it wouldn't work," he said.

"Why not?"

"Angela," Clint explained, "if Trey Hatcher had ridden into town by accident and found that I was here, he and I would be doing this thing tomorrow for free."

"But . . . why?"

"Reputation."

"Is it that important?"

"I don't know," he said. "Why did you leave New Jersey?"

"What do you mean?"

"You wanted to change your life, but you didn't feel you could do it there—not with the reputation you had. Isn't that right?"

"That's exactly right," she said. "I see what you mean."

"Tomorrow morning, first thing," he said, "you ride out to the construction site."

"Why?"

"They need you there to supervise."

"Like hell," she said. "You just don't want me to be here to watch."

"There'll be plenty of people watching," he said. "You can hear about it afterward."

"Maybe I should leave now," she said, starting to sit up.

He wrapped an arm around her waist. "Not a chance."

Chapter Thirty-Five

Trey Hatcher couldn't sleep.

He could never sleep the night before. It had nothing to do with fear; it was the pure *excitement* he felt. The first few times he used to drink, but he quickly realized that drinking would only impede his performance and might get him killed.

After that, he used women, but like the whore who was in his bed now, they usually wore out before he did. He had so much extra energy the night before that no woman was able to keep up with him.

"Jesus, honey," the whore had said earlier, "doesn't that thing *ever* go down?"

As a matter of fact, it didn't. Every time he faced a man with a gun, he had an erection. After he killed one, he always sought out a woman and took care of it. Only then would he find himself satisfied.

"Honey?"

He turned away from the window, naked, and asked, "What is it?"

"I'm ready to try again, if you are."

He turned and faced her fully.

"Oh, I see you *are* ready."

She sat up, a dark-haired woman in her thirties with huge breasts and buttocks. He had simply asked the clerk to send him a woman, and when she appeared at his door he didn't turn her away. One woman was as good as another. The sheet fell away, revealing her big tits and swollen nipples. Whores weren't supposed to want it so bad, but this one did. This one wanted it so bad she was already breathing hard.

"Yeah, I'm ready, sweetheart," he said, walking to the bed. "Take your best shot."

Tom Kennedy looked out the window at the street below. That's where it would happen. He could feel it. Adams and Hatcher would probably step from the hotel together and square off in the street. He could stay right up here and have a front-row seat. First Hatcher would gun down Adams, and then Denver and Beman would take care of Hatcher.

Kennedy would be able to explain that, especially to Sheriff Ransom. Denver and Beman would simply claim that they were trying to help Adams, but they were too slow. He was already dead by the time they got their guns out, and by then they had to shoot to protect themselves. Ransom would buy their story, because Kennedy had bought Ransom a long time ago.

And Kennedy would see it all from here.

He looked at the bed, which he hadn't bothered to turn down, because he knew he'd never get any sleep that night. He'd just sit at that window and play it

over and over in his mind, the way it was supposed
to happen.

The way it *would* happen.

Once Adams was gone, things would get back to
normal. It wouldn't be long before those women
would be only too happy to sell the land to him—
and for a lot less than he had originally offered.

Clint looked down at Angela, who was asleep
beside him. The best was usually worth waiting for,
and she had been the best. Katy and Sandy—they had
simply wanted a man after so long, and he happened
to be handy. Angela, though, had wanted him, and
she had made it well worth the wait.

If this was to be his last night, she had made it a
hell of a night.

And it wasn't over yet.

Chapter Thirty-Six

Tom Kennedy left his room early and found Denver and Beman. He didn't bother to ask them where they had spent the night.

"Set up, one on either side of the street," he told them.

"Sure, Boss."

"And don't miss."

"What about the law?"

"I'm going to see him now. Don't worry about him. Just worry about Hatcher."

Kennedy started walking away until Denver said, "Hey, Boss?"

"Yeah?"

"What do we do if Adams kills Hatcher?"

Kennedy thought it over a moment, then said, "Same thing. Just do the same thing."

Angela was dressed and standing by the window, staring out, when Clint awoke.

"What do you see?" he asked.

"Nothing," she said. "Will you have time for breakfast?"

"I don't think so," he said. "I'd like to get this over with as soon as possible. When will you start back to your place?"

"I'm not," she said.

He was up, already getting dressed. "What do you mean?" he asked.

"I'm staying," she said. "To watch."

"Why?"

She shrugged. "It'll be something to tell my grandchildren."

He strapped on his gun and said, "Is there any way I can talk you out of it?"

"Not unless you want a fight on your hands."

"All right," he said. "You can see the street from here. Don't leave the room, all right?"

"Sure," she said, hugging and rubbing her arms as if she were cold.

He walked to the door and put his hand on the doorknob.

"Should I say 'good luck,' " she asked, "or 'be careful'?"

"Either one."

She waved him away. "Consider them both said."

"When this is over," he said, "we'll have breakfast and then go out and see how the house is coming."

"Sure," she said again.

He opened the door and stepped out into the hall, wondering what would happen if he ran into Hatcher there. Would they have it out right in the hall? Luckily, the hall was empty, and he went downstairs.

*   *   *

"What are you gonna do?" Ransom asked Kennedy.

"I'm going to solve my problems—that's what I'm going to do," Kennedy said. "Just stay here in your office until you hear the shooting. But don't come out until the shooting is over. You understand?"

"Sure, Mr. Kennedy," the sheriff said. "I understand."

When Trey Hatcher awoke, he kicked the whore out of bed.

"Hey!"

"Get out."

"What's wrong with you?" she asked, assuming a hurt look.

"I'm finished with you," Hatcher said.

He grabbed his pants, took out some money, and handed it to her.

"Hey, this is too much," she said.

"Take it and get out."

"Sure, honey," she said, getting dressed. At the door she paused and said, "If you want me again—"

"I'll let you know."

She gave him a smile that was full of promise and left.

Hatcher dressed and strapped on his gun. He couldn't see the street from his room, but he knew there'd be people out there, watching, waiting for something to happen.

He wasn't about to disappoint them.

Clint walked out the front door of the hotel and almost walked into Tom Kennedy.

"Better get yourself a good seat, Kennedy."

"There was an easier way to do this, Adams."

"Was there?"

"Yes."

"Maybe there still is," Clint said.

"No, it's too late now."

"I thought you'd say that."

"When you're gone," Kennedy said, "who's going to stick up for those women, huh?"

"Don't worry about that, Kennedy," Clint said, "because I'm not going anywhere. Not today."

"We'll see."

Kennedy entered the hotel, and Clint stepped down into the street. He saw Walt Denver and his partner immediately, one on either side of the street, and he knew what they were there for.

When Trey Hatcher stepped into the street, Kennedy and Angela were at their windows, watching.

Clint was across the street, leaning against a post.

"Good move, Clint," Hatcher said. "Why drag it out, huh?"

Clint stepped into the street and started walking toward Hatcher.

"Before you go for your gun," he said, "look around. Your employer has a man on each side of the street."

They were close enough that Clint didn't have to yell. He doubted that Walt Denver and the other man could hear them.

"What do you mean?"

"Take a look, but don't make it obvious."

Hatcher looked and saw what Clint was talking about.

"Whichever one of us wins," Clint said, "loses."

"Kennedy would do that?"

"You've talked to him," Clint said. "What do you think?"

Hatcher thought a moment. "Yeah, I guess he would."

Clint looked up and saw Angela standing in the window. Two rooms to the right, he saw Kennedy.

"He's watching now, waiting."

"Walk down to the end of the street, Clint," Hatcher said.

"Trey—"

"We'll take them out first, and then we'll do what we have to do," Hatcher said. "You take the one on your right."

"You're still going to work for him, huh?"

"I'm working for myself."

"If you kill me, you'll be doing him a favor."

Hatcher hesitated, then said, "Walk down to the end of the street."

Clint stared at Hatcher for a few moments, then turned and walked down to the end of the street. When he had gone far enough, he turned.

There were other people on the street on both sides, and still others were rushing to watch. Clint had always hated this—putting on a show for a crowd that was desperate to see some blood.

"Ready?" Hatcher called.

"After you."

Clint watched Hatcher, and for the split second

before the man went for his gun, he wondered if he hadn't been duped. Maybe all three men were there for him, and Hatcher was in on it.

He pushed that thought from his mind as Hatcher moved, and he drew his own gun.

He turned to the right and saw Walt Denver with his gun out. There were people around him, and they panicked and ran when they realized what was happening.

Clint heard a shot, but he concentrated on Denver. The man didn't seem to know what was going on. Adams and Hatcher were supposed to be facing each other.

Tom Kennedy stared down at the street and wondered what the hell was going on.

"Sonofabitch!" he said, drawing his own gun.

He tried to open the window, but it was stuck.

"Shit!" he said, and he shattered one of the panes.

Clint couldn't wait any longer.

"Denver, drop it!" he shouted, but his voice only galvanized the man into action. He pointed his gun at Clint, but Clint fired first. The impact of the bullet knocked the man through a plate-glass window.

He turned quickly and saw that Hatcher had dispatched the other man with no trouble. They looked at each other, but suddenly they heard glass breaking. They both turned and looked up at the hotel window, where Tom Kennedy stood with a gun. Kennedy was trying to decide who to fire at, but he never got the chance. Both Hatcher and Clint fired, and both bullets smacked home.

Now the street was empty. The onlookers had fled, Denver and his partner were dead, and, more than likely, so was Kennedy.

"Now it's just me and you, Clint."

"Trey—" he said, but Hatcher had holstered his gun and wasn't budging from the street.

"Shit!" Clint said, and he holstered his gun.

Chapter Thirty-Seven

"You were right," Clint said to Angela, "it's more than I expected, too."

The house wasn't done, but he could see that it was going to be a one-story structure with at least four rooms.

"It's going to take a couple of days longer to finish," Angela said, "but we can wait. I don't know how to thank Pevy and his men—and you."

Clint looked over to where Pevy stood with his arm around Alice Williams. There were enough men present that Katy and Sandy and even Bonnie and Irene could have their pick.

"It looks to me like the thank-yous will be taken care of."

"You know, I was never so scared," she said. "I mean, not during all the shooting that was done, but when you and Hatcher were facing each other, I was never so scared. Even though it was yesterday, I can still feel the fear."

"I'm always scared."

"What made him do it?" she asked. "What made him walk away like that?"

Clint shrugged. "I'd like to think he just decided to make the smart decision."

She turned to face Clint. "Do you have to leave?"

"It's time, Angela," Clint said.

She leaned into him and kissed him warmly. "Thank you, for everything."

"It was my pleasure, Angela," he said. Then he added, "Well, *most* of it was."

He mounted Duke and looked at the house again.

"You'll be this way again sometime, won't you?" she asked. "To see Beverly?"

"Probably."

"Stop in on us," she said. "Just to say hello."

"I will, Angela."

As Clint rode off, he thought about Hatcher just turning and walking away. He knew Trey Hatcher wasn't afraid of him; so why *had* he decided to call it off?

Maybe they'd cross paths again in the future, and he'd ask him.

Maybe.

TRACKER *series*
by
Award-Winning Author
Robert J. Randisi (J.R. Roberts)

Visit us at www.speakingvolumes.us

GREAT BOOKS

E-BOOKS

AUDIOBOOKS

& MORE

Visit us today

www.speakingvolumes.us

www.ingramcontent.com/pod-product-compliance
Lightning Source LLC
Chambersburg PA
CBHW020636250626
47154CB00008B/2706